THE
SAILOR'S
PROMISE

Part 1
of
The Windsor Street Family Saga

An Introductory Novella

By
VL McBeath

The Sailor's Promise
By VL McBeath

For more about this author please visit
https://valmcbeath.com

For permission requests, write to the author at:
https://vlmcbeath.com/contact/

Editing services provided by Susan Cunningham at Perfect Prose Services
Cover design by Books Covered

ISBNs: 978-1-913838-14-0 (Ebook Edition)
978-1-913838-15-7 (Paperback)

Main category - FICTION / Historical
Other category - FICTION / Sagas

Explanatory Notes

Meal Times

In the United Kingdom, meal times are referred to by a variety of names. Based on traditional working-class practices in northern England in the nineteenth century, the following terms have been used in this book:

Breakfast: The meal eaten upon rising each morning.

Dinner: The meal eaten around midday. This may be a hot or cold meal depending on the day of the week and a person's occupation.

Tea: Not to be confused with the high tea of the aristocracy or the beverage of the same name, tea was the meal eaten at the end of the working day, typically around five or six o'clock. This could either be a hot or cold meal.

Money

In the nineteenth century, the currency in the United Kingdom was Pounds, Shillings and Pence.

- There were twenty shillings to each pound and twelve pence to a shilling.
- A crown and half crown were five shillings and two shillings and sixpence, respectively.
- A guinea was one pound, one shilling (i.e. twenty-one shillings).

For further information on Victorian England visit: https://valmcbeath.com/victorian-era

Please note: This book is written in UK English

CHAPTER 1

January 1871

Nell sat back on her heels, rubbing her hands in front of the range as the fire roared back to life.

"That should warm you up." Her nephew James smiled at her as he took a seat in the armchair to her left.

"I hope so." She sighed and pushed herself to her feet.

"What's the matter? You don't sound very happy."

"Oh, it's nothing. I just hate feeling trapped in the house. I'll be glad to see the back of winter this year."

"You and me both." He reached for the letter opener and sliced the top of an envelope he was carrying.

"What have you got there?"

His face lit up as he read the single page of handwritten text. "It's a letter from the shipping company. They want me to go for an interview next week."

"An interview, that's wonderful. I didn't even know you'd approached them." A grin crossed her face. "Will you go?"

"I'm not sure. I want to, but..." The smile slipped as his hazel eyes stared up at her. "You know what Mam and Dad are like. They'll be mad with me if I do."

Nell watched as he reread the letter. "Why did you apply for a job in the first place, then?"

"I don't know. I was angry at work a couple of weeks ago and thought it would be a good idea..."

"But now you don't?" Nell raised an eyebrow as she took the seat on the opposite side of the fire.

"How can I?" He rested his head on the back of the chair, disturbing his neatly combed ginger hair. "If it wasn't for Dad, I'd be off like a shot, but he'll be home in a couple of weeks, so it's not that easy."

"It's a shame they won't let you make up your own mind."

"Don't I know it." James grimaced. "To hear Dad going on, you'd think I was a freak for wanting to be a steward, but it's a well-paid job. Is it wrong to want to see the world?"

Nell shook her head. "I don't think so ... and your dad should understand. He's been going to sea for years."

"Ah, but according to him, being a ship's carpenter is a manly job. Serving toffs who've got more money than they know what to do with, isn't."

"Well, don't give up." Nell gave him a weak smile. "You're still only sixteen, and once you come of age, you'll be able to make your own decisions. You've plenty of time."

"It's such a long way off, though."

"I know, but at least you have the opportunity to go to sea. I'd love to travel, but unless I marry a rich husband, it's never going to happen."

"But you're a woman; it's different for you." He sighed as he scanned the letter again. "Do you think I should go for the interview?"

"Can you get time off work?"

James nodded. "I can sneak out."

"Then why not? It will be good practice at least, and you never know."

"What if I get the job?" His eyes were wide as he stared at her.

"Then you can decide what you want to do. You won't have to take it, if you're not ready."

"Oh, I'm ready..."

"Listen, why not make some enquiries before your dad comes home? There can't be any harm in asking, can there?"

"You're right." James nodded as if convincing himself. "I need to stand up to him and tell him I don't want to do the same job as him for the rest of my life."

A smile spread across Nell's lips as she leaned back in her chair. "Wouldn't it be wonderful if they took you on? I may not be able to go to sea myself, but if you went, at least I'd be able to see the world through your eyes. You could come back with stories of what life's like in all the exotic places I can only read about. Make sure you capture all the details, mind." She paused to study him. "That way you'll know I'll always be pleased to see you."

James' face brightened. "I can see it all already, but it won't just be the places I'll be able to tell you about. If I'm a steward for the first-class passengers, I'm sure there'll be plenty of tales to tell. Imagine being able to see how the other half lives..." He flinched and sat up straight as the front door opened and an icy blast rushed into the living room.

"Here, let me help you." Nell jumped up and hurried to take the shopping basket off her sister Maria, while she coaxed her daughter Alice into the house.

"I can manage, I've been doing it long enough." Maria slammed the door behind her. "Blimey, it's cold out there." She pushed Alice towards the fire and rubbed her own hands together, stamping her feet on the small rug in front of the hearth as she did. "I'll need to get myself some new boots if the weather carries on like this; these will need resoling at the very least."

"Did you get all the shopping?" Nell rummaged through the basket.

"Most of it. Rebecca carried on to the draper's for more thread, but I was too cold." Maria indicated to the top of the range. "Is there water in that kettle? I'll need a cup of tea before I do anything else; I'm sure Rebecca will, too."

"I'll top it up." Nell collected the kettle on her way to the small scullery off the back corner of the room. When she returned, Maria was standing over her eldest son.

"What have you got there?" She stared down at the letter resting on his knee.

"Oh nothing. A letter from a mate, that's all." James stood up and pushed it into his pocket. "If you don't mind, I'm going to the alehouse for a quick drink before dinner. I'll see you both later."

"Well, don't be late ... and tell our Billy and Vernon to be on time if you see them on the way." Maria shuddered as James opened and closed the front door. "They'll be freezing when they come in."

"They'll be fine; they don't feel the cold like we do." A smile flitted across Nell's lips as she picked up a large wooden spatula and thrust it into a pan of meat and vegetables beside the kettle. "This smells good and at least it won't spoil."

"Here, Aunty Nell."

Nell looked down to see her niece holding a loaf of bread. "There's a good girl. Would you like to go with Mam and put it in the pantry?"

Alice nodded and Maria put a hand on the child's back and guided her to the scullery as Nell replaced the lid on the pan.

"I need to get myself cleaned up." She brushed the soot from her apron. "I'll never find a rich husband dressed like this."

"A rich husband?" Maria reappeared from the pantry. "What are you talking about?"

"Oh, nothing. I was just daydreaming with James about going to sea..."

"Well, you can forget that idea, and don't you go encouraging James, either." Maria shot her a glance. "You know perfectly well what George thinks of him going away, and I don't want any trouble when he gets home."

Nell took a deep breath. "I'm not encouraging him, but don't you think he should decide for himself?"

"No, I don't. It's bad enough having George away for months at a time; I won't have my eldest son going to sea, too." Maria bustled to the front door to hang up her cloak. "Besides, he's tied into his apprenticeship for the next five years, so that's the end of it."

Nell picked up the teapot from the table in the opposite

corner of the room. "I suppose so, but it's such a long time for him to wait."

"He won't be waiting for anything. By the time he's finished, I hope he's old enough to see sense. Now, if you're going to change that skirt, give me that teapot and when you come back, I don't want to hear another word about it."

CHAPTER 2

Second Mate Jack Riley stepped off the gangplank and pulled his coat tightly around him. The wind wasn't as severe as those he'd endured in the southern oceans over the winter, but at the moment, it was giving them a run for their money. Despite his heavy boots, the ground was slippy underfoot, and he took his time walking along the footpath that ran parallel to the docks. He paused, hoping for his first glimpse of Parliament Street. There it was. The road that would take him home. Well, he said home. He was hoping there'd be an empty bed for him in the house on Windsor Street. He'd written to tell the landlady he'd be back, and could only hope she'd given someone else the push if the place was full. If not, he guessed he'd be looking for lodgings this afternoon. Still, it wouldn't be for long. In a few weeks he'd be off again, and he couldn't blame Mrs Duffy for wanting to keep someone else in the room to pay the bills.

As he turned into Parliament Street, the breeze dropped. Not that it was any warmer, but it made walking easier. The road looked as if it hadn't been cleaned for days, and he picked his way through the horse muck covering the cobbles. At least it was winter. He remembered last time he'd been home over the summer; it hadn't been pleasant.

The climb was steady as he crossed over into Upper Parliament Street, and he soon arrived on the corner of Windsor Street. *Right, let's see if I'm welcome.* He took a deep breath as he headed for the house, but stopped when he reached the steps up to the front door. He may have been away for the best part of a year, but how many more houses had they built? He could no longer see fields at the bottom of the road. He shrugged. *I suppose they're necessary with the docks still growing. The newcomers need somewhere to live.*

He climbed the steps and pushed on the front door, thankful it was unlocked, and let himself in.

"Keep that door shut!" A woman's shrill voice shouted from a room at the end of the hall. Jack dropped his duffel bag and popped his head around the door. "It's only me, Mrs D. May I come in?"

His landlady, a middle-aged woman with greying hair and an ample bosom, glanced up from her knitting and scowled at him. "I'd almost given up on you."

Jack walked in and gave her his usual cheery smile. "What a lovely welcome. It's nice to see you too."

Mrs Duffy remained unmoved. "Don't come here with any of your cheek. How long are you back for this time?"

"Until March." He studied the table in the corner of the room. "Is there any tea in that pot?"

She sighed as she pushed herself from her chair. "Give

me a minute and I'll get you one. Have you any rent for me?"

Jack produced a handful of coins from his inside pocket. "It's all here; I've not even been to the alehouse yet. How much would you like?"

A smile crept over Mrs Duffy's face as she stepped forward to inspect the money. "A shilling a week to you."

"A shilling! Are you trying to bankrupt me?"

"You should be grateful; I could have let that bed twice over if I hadn't been saving it for you."

Jack laughed and put an arm around her shoulder. "I bet you could. Where else would folks get such a welcoming smile and friendly banter?"

Mrs D flicked a hand at him. "We'll have less of that. Take a seat at the table and I'll get you something to eat."

If Jack ever wondered why he always came back to this insignificant boarding house, he only needed a plate of scouse to answer his question. There were more potatoes and carrots in it than anything else, but you could find pieces of meat if you looked closely, which he considered a bonus.

Mrs Duffy retook her seat by the fire as Jack attacked his food. He ate without pausing for breath, and with a final wipe of bread around his plate, he arranged his knife and fork neatly and pushed it away.

"My, Mrs D, that was something after being away all this time. What's for pudding?"

Without a word, his landlady disappeared and returned

to place a bowl in front of him. "Treacle sponge and custard. I left it to cool while you were eating."

Jack didn't wait for the pleasantries and dived in with his spoon. Two minutes later, with the bowl empty, he sat back in his chair. "That was smashing. It should set me up for the rest of the day."

Mrs Duffy stood up as he finished his cup of tea. "What are you doing this afternoon?"

Jack shrugged. "Not much. I'll take my bag upstairs and then call into the alehouse to see who's around." He stood up and pushed his chair under the table. "Which room am I in?"

"The back room on the first floor. You'll find the empty bed in the corner with the sheets folded on top."

"Do I have any room-mates?"

"Two other sailors. One leaves next week, the other only arrived the other day. They're both out at the moment."

"We should have something in common then, and they should know how to keep the place tidy." He gave a salute as he opened the door. "I'll see you later."

The room was exactly as he remembered from when he'd last stayed here. Three single beds, each pushed into a corner with two small wardrobes and a washstand. He threw his bag on the bed. It was a good job he travelled light.

Having been a sailor for over twelve years, he was well practised at making his own bed, and five minutes after walking into the room, he let himself out. There'd be plenty of time to rest later.

Mercifully, the walk to the alehouse was short, but with ice still on the ground, he smiled to see a fire roaring in the grate.

"Afternoon, Mr Riley." A large man with a balding head and a full beard stood behind the bar, wiping the mahogany top. "Not seen you for a while. Where've you been?"

Jack walked across to him. "Afternoon, Eric. A pint of the best, please, and have one yourself. I'm just back from the Far East and it was warmer there, I can tell you."

Eric shuddered. "It must have been treacherous crossing that Bay of Biscay at this time of year."

Jack accepted the tankard of ale and pushed a penny across the bar. "It wasn't easy, although we got a move on with all the wind. Have I missed much while I've been gone?"

Eric shook his head. "Not a lot. More houses going up, but then there's nothing unusual in that nowadays."

An icy blast announced the arrival of more customers, and Jack picked up his tankard and carried it to a table near the fire.

"Room for another one?" He sat at a table with two men who were finishing a game of dominos.

"Jack Riley, how are you doing?" The older of the two, a tall man with receding dark hair and a thick beard, offered Jack his hand.

"Good grief, Tom Parry, it's good to see you again."

Tom indicated to the young man beside him. "You know my nephew James, don't you?"

Jack offered James his hand. "Of course, although I've not seen you in here before."

James laughed. "Uncle Tom thought it was about time, and I'd rather be here than at home with me mam."

"Don't you be too hard on her, I'm sure she means well." Jack's smile didn't reach his eyes as he saw an image of his own mam. It was funny how he'd only appreciated her after she'd gone.

James appeared not to notice. "You may be right, but my Aunties Nell and Rebecca are always there and, well ... there's only so much women's talk a man can put up with."

"Ah, yes." Jack laughed and gave James his full attention. "How is your Aunty Nell?"

"She's fine, the same as usual, I suppose. Will you pay her a visit later?"

Jack took a large gulp of ale. "I don't think so. I imagine she's married by now."

"No, she's not." Tom smirked at him. "She's not walking out with anyone either."

Jack said nothing as he watched Tom lay the dominos face down on the table, ready for them to select their pieces. "How come you're not working?"

"We finish at two on Saturdays."

Jack's eyes flitted between the two men. "Since when's that been a thing?"

"Since we heard the millworkers have been given it. Not that it's official..."

"It's all right for some. We never get any time off on the ships; the sea's a cruel mistress."

"It's your choice." Tom raised an eyebrow as he stood his seven dominos on their sides in front of him. "It must be in your blood if you keep going back for more."

Jack placed the double six in the centre of the table. "You get used to it, and what else would I do? I'm going to take my exams while I'm here, so hopefully, I'll be a first mate by the time I leave. It will make life a little easier.

Well, I'll get a nicer bunk at any rate." He grinned at James, who was staring at him. "Do you work, James?"

The young boy grimaced. "I'm apprenticed to be a carpenter, like me dad, but I'd rather go to sea."

Jack studied him. "You can be a ship's carpenter once you qualify. That will take you all over the world."

"That's what me dad does, but it's not for me. I'd rather work on a passenger liner ... as a steward."

Jack raised an eyebrow. "How old are you?"

"Sixteen."

"I imagine you'll be tied to your master for another few years yet, then."

"He's hoping to get out of it." Tom didn't take his eyes off the table. "Not that his dad will be pleased. I've promised not to say anything."

"I can imagine." Jack scanned his dominos for a match before picking up a new one.

"Do you know me dad?" James' smile dropped.

"I've met him a few times. He's nice enough, if I remember rightly. Is he home at the moment?"

"No, but he's due next week." James twisted a domino in his fingers. "You won't say anything to him, will you? About me being a steward."

"Not if you don't want me to. Doesn't he know what you want to do?"

James gulped. "I mentioned it last time he was home, but he went berserk. Said I'd better not get any ideas, or he'd take his belt and beat it out of me."

Jack flinched. "Far be it from me to say anything then. Perhaps you should let him think you'll go to sea as a carpenter."

James' shoulders sagged. "Then I'll have me mam after me."

Jack tapped a finger against the side of his nose. "The best thing you can do then is say nothing. It's easier to ask for forgiveness than permission. Trust me. I know."

CHAPTER 3

The temperature had finally returned to normal after days of snow and arctic winds. Not that there was any sign of the ice on the inside of the windows starting to thaw.

"Another month and this should be gone." Nell squeezed out the cloth into a bucket. "I hope so at any rate; these windows won't last until next winter, if the water keeps getting in."

Maria fastened her young daughter into her coat. "It's about time we moved on. This house isn't big enough now the boys are growing, it's getting to be a squeeze."

Nell was about to point out that if James got the job he wanted, there would be more room, but she bit her tongue. Heaven help her if she was the one to tell Maria of his plans.

"We can think about that when it happens. I imagine you'll need George's permission first; he won't be happy if you move without telling him."

"He'll be back by the end of the week." Maria grinned.

"I'll have to get in his good books if I want him to pay a higher rent, given he's hardly ever here."

Nell peered out of the front window. "I'm sure he'll understand. At least James is working, so we have more money coming in."

"He is for now, but I don't like him spending so much time with that brother of ours. He's a bad influence on him, missing work as often as he does. He should be setting a good example."

"He doesn't do it on purpose. It's the cold weather that's the problem. It hurts his joints."

"I don't believe a word. It's nothing but an excuse." Maria took her cloak from the hook by the door. "There are men who work in much worse conditions than him, and you never hear them complaining. Right, I'll be going."

Nell turned back from the window. "May I walk to the shop with you? Other than nipping to the privy and the ash pit, I've not been out for weeks. I could do with stretching my legs. We can ask Rebecca, too."

Maria tutted as she fastened the ribbon of Alice's bonnet under her chin. "You'd better hurry up then. I haven't got time to stand around waiting."

"Rebecca." Nell called up the stairs. "Would you like to walk to the shops with us?"

The dusty face of Nell's sister appeared over the handrail. "Now?"

"Yes. Maria's about to leave, so you'll need to be quick."

Rebecca looked down at the soot stains on the front of her dress. "I'd better not. I need to finish the fires and then do the mending for that woman on Parliament Street. I'll be in trouble if I don't collect the money this afternoon."

"Ah yes, I'd forgotten."

"Lucky you, I wish I could. I need to sort myself out for this evening, too."

Nell grinned. "Mr Grayson. I'm not surprised that walking out with him is more important than coming with us. I'll see you later."

"You'll understand one of these days."

Nell sighed. *I already do.* She reached for her cloak as Maria picked up the well-worn shopping basket with one hand and grabbed Alice's arm with the other.

"We'll start walking, I've not got all day. You can catch us up."

Thankful she could pull her hat over her ears, without the need for a hat pin, Nell fastened her cloak and hurried to the front door, slamming it behind her as she raced to catch her sister up. "Can we go the long way round? I'd like to get some fresh air."

Maria shook her head and scowled. "And be even later arriving at the shop? They don't keep things back for me, you know."

Nell's smile faded. "Sorry, I didn't think of that."

"No, well it's time you did."

Nell folded her arms under her cloak. "I would if you let me, I'm not a child any more. I'd do all the shopping, but you don't want me to."

Maria's voice softened. "There's no need for that. I'll tell you what, we can take the long way home. The meat won't go off in this weather."

Nell relaxed and took a deep breath, the saltiness of the sea air filling her lungs. "I'd like that."

. . .

The grocery store on Windsor Street was no more than a five-minute walk, and as they reached the junction at the top of their road and turned left, the striped awning came into view.

"I'll wait outside with Alice if you like," Nell said as they approached the shop. "It's nice being in the air."

"As you wish; I won't be long."

As soon as the door closed behind Maria, Alice dropped the ball she'd been clutching and ran to catch it.

"Alice, come back." Nell lunged after her and put her foot on the ball to save it from falling into the road.

"That was well stopped."

Nell spun around to see her brother looking down at her. "What are you doing here?"

Tom glanced over the top of Nell's head towards the alehouse further up the road. "They didn't have any work for me today; I'll go in tomorrow."

"How can they be short of work? They always need barrels making."

Tom shrugged. "Not today. What are you doing here, anyway?"

"I wanted to take some air; I've not been out much since it snowed and..." She stopped as a young man with dark eyes and unkempt hair protruding from his cap approached.

"Morning, Nell."

"Jack. I-I didn't know you were back."

"Begging your pardon." He gave a mock bow. "I wasn't aware I had to tell you."

"Well, no, you had no reason to. When did you arrive?"

"Last Saturday." Jack smirked as he turned to Tom. "You're early this morning."

"I could say the same about you, especially if you're heading straight for the alehouse."

"No, not yet. I've a few things to do first." He checked his pocket watch. "I'd better get a move on."

"I'll come with you; I'm heading that way myself." Tom turned to leave, but Jack winked at Nell, his eyes carrying a hint of mischief.

"I expect I'll see you around."

"I-I expect so. How long are you home for?" Nell stammered over her words. *What's the matter with me?*

"A couple of months. I don't have a definite date yet."

"Yes, well, I'm sure I'll see you then."

"Come on, Jack. I thought you were in a hurry." Tom had already moved away, but he gave Nell one last look. "Not a word to Maria." He hadn't taken a step when the shop door opened and his sister appeared.

"Not so fast, Tom Parry. Why aren't you in work again?"

A dark cloud passed over Tom's face. "I don't have to answer to you."

Maria put her basket on the footpath. "It's about time you answered to someone. Does Sarah know you're not working today?"

Tom's eyes flicked to Jack before they settled on Maria. "Of course she does."

"And how's she going to feed a family of six when you're not earning any money? It doesn't grow on trees."

His piercing black eyes narrowed. "I'm perfectly capable of providing for my family, and so I'd ask you to mind your own business." Tom put a hand on Jack's shoulder. "Now, if you'll excuse us."

"Don't you go encouraging him, Jack Riley. I know what you're like." Maria stood with her hands on her hips as the two men disappeared around the corner onto Upper Parliament Street. "He's got a cheek. Poor Sarah's worried sick about stretching out the housekeeping to feed those kiddies, and there's him, swanning off around town and drinking half the money he does earn."

"Come on, don't upset yourself." Nell gave her sister a sideways glance as they started walking. "You shouldn't blame Jack though; he's only been back a few days."

Maria glared at her. "Don't you go getting any ideas about him. You know how upset you were last year, when he built up your hopes about settling down and then left you to go back to sea. I don't want to see you like that again."

"That wasn't his fault..."

"Well, it certainly wasn't yours. You need to find yourself someone like Mr Grayson. He won't go running off to sea as and when he feels like it."

Nell gave a low murmur. She was well aware of that. *Curse you, Jack. Why do you do this to me?*

CHAPTER 4

Nell picked a cloth from her bucket and squeezed it out. George was due back any day now, and Maria insisted they clean the house from top to bottom before he arrived. She peered at the black mould on the wood between the panes of glass in the window. It wouldn't be easy to get rid of it while the ice was still thick.

She pulled the foot stool across the window and was about to step on when a familiar figure walked past. *Jack.* After turning round to check she was alone, she hurried to the front door, staring down the street in the direction he was heading. When there was no sign of him, she stopped to scratch her head. *Where is he? He can't have gone far.* She searched in the opposite direction as she turned to go into the house. *Maybe he'll be back.* She plonked her hands on her hips and studied the window. *It would look so much better if it was cleaned on the outside too.*

Despite wearing her heavy cloak, Nell's hands were numb as she polished the outside of the glass. Not for the first time, she looked around. *Come on, Jack, where are you?*

I can't stay outside much longer. Maria was now sweeping the living room floor and was bound to notice how slowly she was working.

She shivered and stamped her feet. Why was she behaving like this? Even if he came back, what would she say to him? They hadn't parted on the best of terms last time he'd gone to sea, but knowing he was around again...

"What are you doing out there?" Maria popped her head through the door. "You must be freezing and it'll be dark if you don't get a move on."

"I'm coming. I wanted to make sure there were no streaks on the glass."

"With ice still on the inside, nobody would notice even if there were. Leave it for now, I need this table setting before James gets home."

Nell picked up her bucket and threw the dirty water into the gutter. With a last glance down the street, she stepped into the living room.

"There we are, all done." She crossed the room to the back door and put the bucket in the yard. "Let me fetch the stool then I'll get the table set."

"Well, hurry up. I don't know what's got into you." Maria was on her hands and knees, scrubbing at a stain on the wall. "James will be home soon. Give the other two a shout if you see them."

Once at the front door Nell scanned the street looking for her young nephews, but she couldn't see them anywhere. *They'll be back in a minute. It's not like them to miss a meal.* She went outside and picked up the stool, but as she was about to go into the house James appeared at the top of the road. *Goodness,*

I'm in trouble now. She put a hand on the door frame but stopped when a second figure rounded the corner. *Jack.* She hesitated. *I need an excuse. I'll pretend I'm looking for the boys.*

Leaving the stool beside the front door, she wandered to the nearest corner and peered down the street.

"Are you after our Billy and Vernon?" James waved as he called to her.

"Yes, have you seen them?"

"They're on Park Road, they'll be here in a minute."

"Oh, good." Nell waited for them to join her, her stomach churning.

"Good afternoon, Nell." Jack's teeth were perfect as he smiled at her.

"Jack. Twice in one day. What have you been doing with yourself?" Her cheeks flushed.

"A bit of this and that. Nothing of interest."

Her eyes flicked to James, hoping he would leave them, but he stayed where he was.

"What have you been doing, Aunty Nell?"

"Not much, mainly cleaning, ready for your dad coming home."

"When's he due?" Jack looked at James.

"Tomorrow."

"That's nice. I've not seen him for years."

James grimaced. "Besides me mam, you're probably the only one who's looking forward to seeing him."

"I'm sure Billy and Vernon are; Vernon especially." Nell forced a smile.

"I don't know why."

Jack slapped James on the back. "Don't let it worry you.

I imagine he'll spend most of his time in the alehouse, so you'll hardly see him."

"I hope you're right." James sighed as he took Nell's arm. "Come on, Aunty Nell. Let's make the most of our last night without him."

As the clock struck half past five, Nell placed the last two plates of cooked meat and cheese onto the table and stepped back to check she hadn't forgotten anything.

"Are we done?"

Nell nodded as Maria walked past with the teapot and called everyone to sit down. Billy and Vernon were the first to arrive and jostled to sit at the head of the table, but in an instant, James caught them both by the arm.

"Behave yourselves. You know where you sit." He pushed them towards the far end of the table where Nell had already seated Alice.

"Where's Rebecca? She should be ready by now."

Maria rolled her eyes. "This liaison with Mr Grayson's getting rather serious."

Billy and Vernon giggled as they nudged each other.

"Will you two behave? I don't know what's got into you tonight." Maria clipped the two of them around the ears on her way to the foot of the stairs. "Rebecca, are you coming?"

"Yes, I'm here." She hurried down the stairs. "Don't wait for me, I want to fix my hat before I sit down."

"Don't be surprised if there's nothing left. What have you been doing?"

"Don't be like that. It took me longer than I thought to

24

finish that hemming. You were happy enough to take the money."

"You should know how long it takes to do these jobs; you've been doing it long enough."

"The skirt was wider than I expected. Honestly, who still wears a crinoline in this day and age? Besides, I needed to get myself ready. Mr Grayson will be here in half an hour."

"I suggest you come and sit down then. You won't be able to fuss about when George is back."

Nell looked at her sister's pretty face, framed with ringlets, and sighed. Maria was right. He was a stickler for punctuality and decorum at the table. She'd have to move faster if she didn't want to upset him.

"Do we know he's definitely arriving tomorrow?" Rebecca asked.

"He is, I checked the timetable myself." James helped himself to some bread. "Before he gets here, though, I have some news of my own." He smirked at Nell.

"What sort of news?" Maria put down the knife and fork she'd just picked up. "Shouldn't you wait to tell Dad first?"

"I thought you'd be interested." He took a deep breath. "I've got a new job."

Nell's eyes widened as Maria glared at him. "You've already got a job."

"He hates it." Billy nudged Vernon as his younger brother giggled. "He wants to be a servant."

"A steward." James gritted his teeth.

"Oh, yes," Billy mumbled as he laughed into a glass of milk.

"I don't think so." Maria's chest heaved. "Dad told you last year what he thought of that idea, and I won't have you upsetting him."

"It's not my fault he doesn't understand..."

Maria banged a hand on the table. "While Dad puts a roof over your head, you'll do as you're told. Now not another word about this. Are you listening?"

Rebecca had hardly touched her food, and as James sat with a sullen face, she excused herself from the table.

"Mr Grayson will be here in a minute. I need to get my cloak."

Nell sprang from her own seat. "I'll top up the teapot." She picked up the kettle and hurried to the scullery but took her time filling it with water and putting it back on the range.

The winter sun had long since gone, but with James and Maria arguing, she pulled her shawl more tightly around her shoulders and stepped outside. She shivered at the cold, but the moon was near full and so she wandered to the end of the privy and rested against the wall, fixing her gaze on the stars. She hadn't been there a minute when the sound of footsteps disturbed her.

"Oh, it's you. I thought your mam was looking for me."

"Not yet." James wandered to the space beside her. "Why can't she be like you and understand?"

Nell squeezed his hand. "Don't be too hard on her, I guess she's worried about what your dad will say. You know what he's like."

"But it's so unfair. I'm sixteen ... I should be able to choose what I do for the rest of my life."

"Once you come of age, they'll have less say over you. It

might give your dad chance to get used to the idea, too."

James snorted. "I doubt it. Mam told me not to mention it."

"Did you accept the job offer?"

James nodded. "I told them I wanted it, but I've not signed anything."

"Perhaps they'll hold it open for you."

"For five years? I wouldn't think so."

Nell sighed. "You're right. Maybe you could go to sea as an apprentice sailor then? It would get you away from here, and I'm sure your dad wouldn't mind that so much."

"*He* might not, but I would."

Nell turned to look at him. "There's no harm in finding out about it. Why don't you talk to Jack? He likes it well enough."

James straightened up and gave her a sly glance. "Is that why you fell out with him?"

"I didn't fall out with him, it was a ... disagreement."

James studied her. "That wasn't what it sounded like to me. He thinks you don't like him any more."

"Did he say that?" Nell's heart skipped a beat.

James nodded. "Pretty much."

Nell gazed up at the moon. "It's not that I don't like him, but he loves the sea too much. You've seen how hard it is for your mam while your dad's away. I don't want to end up like that."

"So you wouldn't consider walking out with him again?" James gazed at the back of the house next door and appeared not to notice Nell hesitate.

"Not unless he gives up the sea ... and that's not going to happen."

CHAPTER 5

Jack shivered as he waited for the alehouse to open. He knew he was early, but what else was there to do in the middle of winter? He checked his pocket watch for the third time in five minutes. It wouldn't be long now. He wrapped his arms around himself and leaned back on the wall, but the sight of Nell walking towards the shop caused him to stand up straight again.

"Good morning." He walked towards her and raised his cap. "They've let you out on your own for a change."

Nell hesitated but flashed him a smile. "Good morning. George will be home shortly and Maria didn't want to be out when he arrived."

Jack smirked. "She's making herself all glamorous, is she?"

"No! She's fussing around the house, if you must know. Now, if you'll excuse me, I need to get to the shop."

Jack stepped to one side to let her pass, but caught hold of her arm as she did. "Before you go, is James all right? I expected to see him in the alehouse last night, but he didn't arrive."

Nell lowered her eyes as he gazed at her. "No, he stayed in. With his dad coming home, you understand..."

"Did he tell his mam about the new job?" Jack studied Nell as her eyes widened.

"He told you?"

Jack nodded. "He asked me what I thought he should do."

Nell glared at him. "And you encouraged him to mention it?"

"No, I didn't." He held up his hands. "I tried to talk him out of it and told him to accept the position and tell them later, but he wanted to test the news on Maria before his dad came home. I take it she wasn't happy."

"She's banned him from mentioning it ever again. Especially to George."

Jack screwed up his face. "Poor chap. We didn't think she'd go that far. Doesn't she like the idea herself, or is she worried about what the old man will say?"

Nell stared past him. "A bit of both, I think. I feel so sorry for him."

"He's lucky to have you on his side. It's ironic, but he told me you're the only one in the family who understands him."

Nell kicked a stone on the footpath as Jack gazed at her. "I suppose I am."

"Would you let him go if you were his mam?"

She shrugged. "Why not? It will do him the world of good, and he'd enjoy it much better than being a carpenter. Do you know how much he hates his current job?"

"I do. We had a chat about it." Jack checked over his shoulder as the bolt on the alehouse door clanged, but stayed where he was. "He thinks going to sea will be much more exciting."

"It won't help that you've got plenty of tales to tell, too. It's bound to unsettle him."

Jack grinned as Nell lowered her eyelashes. "I have, even some you've not heard before. Perhaps we can catch up one afternoon? Or evening?"

"I don't think so." Nell stepped backwards but stopped as Jack cocked his head to one side.

"Why would you be happy for James to go to sea, but not me?"

She pursed her lips as she held his gaze. "You know why."

"I've missed you, Nell."

She lowered her eyes again. "It wasn't me who went to sea for a year."

"I told you; I had no choice. I'd already signed up for the trip and couldn't get out of it. If I'd known you'd be waiting for me, it might have been different."

"But you knew how I felt..." She paused and took a breath. "I imagine you'll be going away again soon."

"Not for weeks yet."

"Weeks pass too quickly." She looked around, wiping her eyes with the back of her hands. "I need someone who works around here. In Toxteth or Liverpool. Someone who'll come home each evening and eat the food I put on the table. Someone who'll be a dad to my children and not be someone they only know by name. You can't give me that, Jack."

He studied his boots. "I'm sorry, Nell."

"I'd better go. Maria will wonder where the milk is. Goodbye, Jack."

Jack stood tall and raised his cap. "Goodbye, Nell." He watched her disappear into the shop, taking a minute before ambling towards the alehouse. He hadn't reached the door when a man with a shock of ginger hair rounded the corner and walked towards him.

"George!" He raised an arm to wave. "I heard you were due back."

George returned the gesture. "Jack Riley, I've not seen you around these parts for a while."

Jack laughed. "Probably because you've not been here. You've just missed Nell. She's doing the shopping so your missus will be home when you arrive."

"Knowing Maria, she'll be rushing with something, panicking that she won't be ready by the time I arrive."

Jack's eyes lit up, and he pointed to the alehouse. "Do you fancy a quick one, then?"

George took out his pocket watch. "Aye, go on. One won't hurt."

"I'm glad you're back." Jack held open the door. "There's never much company in here during the day." He ordered two pints of best ale and wandered to a table by the fireplace where George had perched himself on a stool.

"I'll be here for a few weeks, so we'll have time to put the world to rights. Does Tom still come in?"

"He does. Most evenings and occasionally around midday. It depends if he's working." Jack stepped back to the bar to collect two tankards of ale before returning to the table.

"Good health." George took a large swig of his drink and wiped his lips with the back of his hand. "My, that tastes good. Tom's still up to his old tricks, is he?"

"I'd say so. He's been coming in with your lad, too."

George's brow creased. "Who, James?"

"That's him. Nice lad. Looks a lot like you."

George grunted. "That's about all we've got in common. Tom's not got him skipping work, has he?" His hazel eyes narrowed.

"I don't think so, although he doesn't seem happy at work."

"He doesn't need to be happy, as long as he brings home his wages."

Jack eyed his companion over the rim of his tankard. "Not everyone's cut out to be a carpenter; he may be happier if he worked on the ships."

"He can do that once he's finished his apprenticeship, same as me, but he needs a trade behind him first." George was about to take another slurp of ale when he stopped and stared at Jack. "He's not still going on about being a waiter is he?"

"A waiter? Erm ... no. Not that I know of."

"Good." He drained his tankard and slammed it onto the table. "I'm not having any son of mine kowtowing to that lot. I thought I got the message through last time I was home."

"I-I'm sure you did. He hasn't mentioned it."

"Good. I'll see you later." George stood up and reached for his duffel bag as Jack puffed out his cheeks. *Poor James.*

"You want to watch what you're saying." Eric wandered

over to pick up the empty tankard. "You'll be getting that lad into trouble."

"I was trying to help ... put in a word for him."

"I wouldn't get involved if I was you." Eric nodded to the drink Jack clutched to his chest. "Will you be making that last all day?"

Jack studied his tankard. "No, but I'd better not have another one. Mrs D's expecting me for dinner and I've an appointment this afternoon."

Eric gawked at him. "An appointment?"

"Don't look at me like that, it's not that unusual." He finished his ale and pushed himself up from the stool. "I'll be back later."

With his dinner eaten and Mrs Duffy's suet pudding and custard weighing heavy in his stomach, Jack set off down Upper Parliament Street towards the river. At least he was in good time, which was about the only thing he had going in his favour. Maybe luck would be with him and he'd be able to talk his way through the examination. He scoffed at himself. Who was he kidding?

He reached the office with ten minutes to spare and turned to look at the array of sailors as they loaded and unloaded their cargos. How many times had he done the same thing in ports around the world? Too many. He wanted more than that.

He turned and pushed on the door to the Marine Board, but halted as he bumped into a clerk. "I beg your pardon."

"Mr Riley?"

Jack took off his cap. "Yes, that's me. I'm here for the examination."

"I'm aware of that, sir. We're waiting for you."

Jack's brow creased as he followed the clerk along a long, plain corridor towards a flight of stairs. "I'm not late, am I?"

"The examination started five minutes ago, sir. Didn't you get the letter?"

Jack wiped the palms of his hands on his trousers. "No, I didn't. I was expecting it to start at two o'clock."

The clerk threw open a door to a wood-panelled office with three men sitting at individual desks. "Never mind, you're here now. The question sheet is on the table and the exam will end at a quarter to four."

Jack hurried to the empty chair, and with his cap resting on the corner of the desk, he turned over the paper. Code signals. *Code signals! When did they change that? It should be navigation.* He turned around to study the other men in the room, but they all had their heads down. *Am I the only one who didn't know about this?* He glanced over to the examiner but quickly pulled his pen from his jacket pocket as a pair of bright blue eyes stared at him.

His heart pounded as he read the first question. *How am I supposed to know? The captain did all that on the last trip.* He skipped to the next question and worked as best he could for the next hour and a half. When he finally sat back, with too many questions still unanswered, his shoulders sagged. It would be a miracle if he passed this, but there was nothing he could do about it now. He shook his head. Another twelve months wasted. He needed to take these exams more seriously. Or quit.

As the clock reached a quarter to four, the man at the front of the room, who wore something resembling a uniform, rang a small handbell.

"Thank you, gentlemen. Leave your papers on the desks. We'll notify you of your results in the next few days. In the meantime, the navigation examination will be at the same time next week."

Jack hovered by the door as the other three men left the room.

"May I help you, Mr Riley?"

The naval officer stood up from his desk to collect the papers.

"I didn't get the letter telling me of the change of time or examination. I was expecting navigation."

The man looked unconcerned. "You should have received something on Monday. Everyone else did."

"But I didn't ... and why was it changed?" Jack followed him around the room.

"The registrar sent the wrong papers. We only realised on Friday and so we had to change the time. Don't worry, navigation will be next week. I'll expect a good mark from you for that. Good day, Mr Riley."

Jack ran a hand through his tousled hair. There was no point arguing. He probably should have looked at code signals by now, anyway. At least he'd got some experience of navigation on his last trip, but unless he passed today's paper, it wasn't worth taking the next one. Not if he needed to pass all three. He'd have to hope he'd done enough. He left the building and sat on a step that overlooked the river.

Would it make that much of a difference if I was a first mate rather than a second? He didn't need to think about it.

Yes, it would. A big difference. Besides the money, there'd be no chance of becoming a master mariner if he gave up now. He sighed. *If that's not going to happen, what about settling down and getting a job here?* That required more thought. *Would Nell give me another chance if I did?* He smiled as he pictured her deep brown eyes and the long dark hair she tied neatly on the top of her head. They were such a contrast to her flawless, pale complexion. He jumped up from the step. *She might.* There was only one way to find out.

CHAPTER 6

Maria carried a pan of scouse from the range to the table and stepped back as George took his seat.

"I thought this would go down well after all those months at sea; make you glad to be home."

"I'm always glad to be back." He put an arm around her waist and gave her a squeeze. "A man misses a lot while he's at sea, not just a good plate of food."

"Yes, I'm sure." Her face flushed as she straightened her apron. "Come along, everyone. Dad doesn't want to be kept waiting."

Nell scurried to get the teapot while Rebecca helped Alice to her chair. Without waiting, Maria ladled two large scoops of stew onto George's plate and placed it in front of him.

"You tuck in, there's no point letting it go cold."

"It'll make a change to have something hot." George looked up as his sons took their seats at the table, his gaze flicking to Billy and Vernon.

"How's school?"

"It's all right," Vernon mumbled as he attacked his food.

"It should be more than all right. I hope you're both paying attention; you won't learn anything if you don't."

"It's boring..."

George banged a hand on the table. "That's not the attitude. I want to see good grades from you when I'm next home. What about you?" His eyes rested on Billy.

"I'll be finished school soon."

"I've not forgotten; I need to sort you out an apprenticeship while I'm here." He stopped and took a mouthful of tea. "What do you want to do? Carpentry like your old dad?"

Billy's cheeks reddened. "If you don't mind, can I be a cooper, like Uncle Tom?"

"You've been speaking to him, have you?" He took another mouthful of scouse. "I don't see why not. James has already taken my profession, and barrel-making's a good trade."

Billy's shoulders relaxed as he accepted a plate. "Uncle Tom said he can help."

"If he ever goes into work." Maria put the spoon back into the pan and sat down. "He seems to spend more time in the alehouse than he does on the docks. Poor Sarah's sick with worry..."

"That's enough, he knows what he's doing." George watched James help himself to another piece of bread. "What about you?"

"Me?" James' voice squeaked.

"Yes, you. How's the apprenticeship going? It's not a difficult question."

Maria sucked in her cheeks as she leaned towards

George. "He's gone and got himself another job, That's what he doesn't want to tell you."

Nell's heart skipped a beat as George glared at his son. "Another job? You're tied to that indenture for another four years. You can't up and leave when you feel like it."

"No ... but ... I'm not happy..."

"Happy!" George slammed a hand on the table. "Since when did happy come into it? You get an apprenticeship, learn your trade and earn an honest day's wage until you drop."

"B-but I can earn more money on the ships."

George's face turned puce as he stood up and leaned over James. "Money or not, if you think I'm going to let a son of mine go to sea to do women's work, you can think again."

"It's not women's work..." James' sentence was cut short as George's fist struck the side of his head.

"If I say it's women's work, that's what it is, and I won't have you bowing and scraping to a bunch of toffs who spend more money on a voyage than I earn in a year."

James stood up, rubbing the cut on his temple. "You don't understand. It's not like that..."

"Are you arguing with me?" George reached for his belt to unbuckle it. "If you think I'm going to sit by and watch you walk out on a perfectly good apprenticeship, that cost me a fortune, you can think again."

James' eyes flicked down to the buckle as he stepped backwards from the table and headed for the stairs. "No, I won't ... I promise."

George ran the leather between his gnarled fingers.

"It was a mistake, I'm sorry, please don't..."

George threw the belt to the ground and grabbed James by the arms, shaking him as he did. "You'd better be sorry. If I hear another word about you going on the ships, you won't walk for a week. Do you hear me? I thought I'd made myself clear last time I was at home."

James' face was white. "Yes ... you did. I'm sorry. I-I won't mention it again..."

"Well, see that you don't." George pushed him backwards causing him to fall up the stairs and crash into the wall. He turned round in an instant and picked up his belt, glaring at Billy and Vernon as he did. "You two as well. I expect you to work on the docks, like the rest of the family, and hold your heads up high. Is that clear?"

Without a word, the boys nodded and watched as George refastened his belt and sat back down to finish his tea.

Nell shifted in her chair, thankful she had Alice to her left to distract her. As the silence lingered, she peeped over at James, who had retaken his seat. He bowed his head, and she wondered if he was crying. If he was, he'd better keep it to himself. Beside him, Rebecca pushed the remains of her tea around her plate, but she knew better than to say anything.

George ate the rest of his tea in silence, before he placed his knife and fork back on his plate.

"Did you enjoy that?" Maria rested a hand on his, but immediately removed it when he glared at her. "What am I thinking; would you like another cup of tea?"

George shook his head. "I'm going to the alehouse. At least I can have a decent conversation down there." He pushed himself from his chair and kissed Maria on the top of the head. "I'll see you later."

At the sound of the front door slamming behind him, Nell and the boys sat back in their seats, each taking a deep breath. Even Rebecca was slow to leave the table. Eventually, she stood up.

"I need to go. Mr Grayson will be wondering where I am."

Nell expected the usual titter and nudging from Billy and Vernon, but they sat dumbfounded, only their restless eyes showing signs of life.

"Didn't you tell him George was coming home?" Maria stood up to tidy the table.

"I did, but I didn't think he'd keep us so long." She checked her hat in the mirror. "I'll see you later."

James didn't wait for Rebecca to disappear before he moved to a seat by the fireplace and rubbed a hand across his eyes. "Why are you always so pleased that he's home, when the rest of us want him to leave as soon as he gets here?"

"That's enough, James Atkin." Maria towered over him. "He's your father and deserves some respect around here."

"Why?" James jumped to his feet. "People should earn respect, not expect it because they're a bully."

Nell flinched as Maria pulled back an arm to strike his face, but James caught hold of it.

"Can't you see? He's been home less than four hours and has us at loggerheads already. You're even acting the same as him." He pushed Maria's arm away. "I won't put up with it." He stormed to the door. "I'm going out."

Billy and Vernon sat at the table, not daring to move, but Nell stood up and helped Alice from her chair.

"I'll take her up to bed."

Billy watched as she left the table. "C-can we go out again?" He reached for Vernon's hand as he edged towards the door.

"I want you back in half an hour." Maria stood with her hands on her hips as the room emptied, but Nell didn't wait for permission to leave. With Alice's hand in hers, she hurried upstairs and shut the bedroom door behind her, leaning against it to catch her breath. *What an evening.*

"I don't want to go to bed." Alice sat down on the floor.

"It's bedtime, so be a good girl. Let's get your dress off." Nell struggled as Alice resisted her attempts to pull her arms into her nightdress. "Stop that this minute. Now, into bed." Nell pursed her lips as she held up the covers.

"You stay with me." The child's soft brown eyes pleaded with Nell.

"All right, for a little while, but I need to help Mam."

"Is James hurt?"

Nell bit her lip. "I don't think so. Dad was tired, but I'm sure he'll be back to his usual self tomorrow."

"He shouldn't do that." Alice put her hands over her face. "He's scary."

Nell pulled the covers over Alice's shoulders. "Close your eyes and try not to think about it; Dad won't be home again until late."

Once she knew Alice was asleep, Nell crept down the stairs, to find Maria sitting in a chair by the fireplace, the table still covered in dirty plates.

She looked up as Nell joined her. "Ah, you're here." She groaned and got to her feet. "Come along, we need to get this tidied up."

Nell watched as Maria busied herself. "It's not like you to leave a mess; are you all right?"

"Why wouldn't I be?"

"Because George just terrorised your son, not to mention everyone else in the family, that's why."

Maria paused momentarily. "You have to see it from his point of view; he's angry with James for wanting to give up a perfectly good job and go into service."

"But you shouldn't side with him when he's clearly being a bully."

"Have you forgotten that George is the one who keeps a roof over our heads and so we have to put up with it? I tried to make everything perfect tonight so he'd be happy, but James had to spoil it."

"It was George's reaction that spoiled it … and the fact that you told him in the first place. What were you thinking of?"

Maria stamped her foot. "Don't blame me … or him. He's a good man and had a right to know. Now, get a move on. I don't want to be doing this all night."

Nell carried the dirty dishes to the scullery, where a sink of lukewarm water was waiting. "You sit down, I'll do these. The boys won't be long."

Maria nodded. "They'd better not be. I want them both in bed by half past seven."

Nell raised her eyebrows but said nothing. *That won't go down well.*

. . .

The fire was burning low when Nell opened her eyes to see Maria dozing in the chair opposite. *I must have nodded off.* She sat up straight as Maria stirred.

"What time is it?"

Nell peered at the wooden clock on the mantelpiece. "Just turned ten o'clock. I was about to go upstairs; will you wait up for George?"

Maria rubbed her hands over her face. "He could be another hour yet ... but perhaps I should."

"You'll be exhausted if you sit up every night."

"But tonight's his first night back. I think I should..."

Maria stopped as the front door opened and Rebecca hurried in, her eyes sparkling. "You'll never guess what? Mr Grayson's proposed marriage to me!"

Nell jumped to her feet. "How wonderful." She threw her arms around her sister. "Did he give you a ring?"

Rebecca held out her left hand. "Real rubies set in gold."

Nell held her sister's finger. "It's lovely. Maria, look. When's the happy day?"

"We've not decided..." The smile on Rebecca's lips froze, and she stopped to study Maria. "Aren't you happy for me?"

Maria didn't smile. "Did he ask George?"

"George ... no. He wasn't here, and..."

"He's not your father. Is that what you were going to say?"

"No, I wasn't ... but he's not."

"He's the closest thing you've got, and the one you'll

expect to pay for the wedding." Maria glared at her. "Don't go getting all excited until you have his permission."

The colour drained from Rebecca's cheeks. "H-he asked Tom."

"Tom?" Maria's voice squeaked.

"He is my brother."

"And has he kept you for the last sixteen years since Mam and Dad died? Is he the reason you and Nell were able to go to school? No! George has been more like a father than Tom ever has, and I don't want him being upset because you asked Tom instead of him."

Rebecca sank into the chair Nell had left empty. "I'm sorry, I didn't think."

"No, clearly."

Nell crouched beside her. "I'm sure it will be fine. Now George is home, Mr Grayson can ask him as well."

"But what if he says no?" Panic swirled in Rebecca's eyes.

"Why would he do that? Mr Grayson's a nice enough man, with a good job." Nell scowled at Maria. "You won't let him spoil their plans, will you?"

Maria bristled. "It's not up to me."

"But you can talk to him." When Maria failed to respond, Nell turned back to Rebecca. "What were you going to say about the date?"

"Mr Grayson hasn't booked anything because he wanted me to choose. Isn't that sweet? We've talked of nothing else tonight and thought we'd like it to be in June."

"Of this year?" Maria's voice pierced the air. "That doesn't give George long to save up. We don't even know if he'll be here to give you away."

Rebecca buried her face in her hands. "Why are you being so mean? Didn't we have enough at teatime?"

"I'm sure it won't matter if George is away. Tom can do it." Nell glared at Maria. "Can't he?"

"But it should be George..."

"But if he's not here, Tom's a perfectly good stand-in." Nell's heart was pounding as she waited for Maria to say something.

"I suppose ... but I don't want him upset again."

"Well, we'll have to make sure he isn't." Nell's eyes flicked between her sisters. "Are we agreed? If George is here, he'll give you away, and if not, Tom can do the honours."

"We haven't even asked him yet." Rebecca rocked backwards and forwards as her sobs filled the room. "The mood he's in, he's bound to ruin everything..."

"No, he's not." Nell pulled Maria into the scullery. "What's got into you? Didn't you see the smile on her face when she came in here not five minutes ago and now look at her." She pointed to the living room. "Are you pleased with yourself?"

Maria released her arm from Nell's grip. "I'm going to bed. I don't suppose he'll expect me to stay up."

Nell waited until Maria reached the top of the stairs before she went back to Rebecca. "I'm sure everything will be fine."

Rebecca wiped her eyes. "Why did George have to come home today, of all days?"

Nell sighed. "He had to arrive sometime, but stop worrying. I promise I won't let him or Maria spoil your big day."

CHAPTER 7

George had left the breakfast table by the time Nell arrived downstairs the following morning.

"He was out quickly." She nodded towards the empty chair as she sat next to Maria.

"He said he had things to do. No idea what though."

Nell poured some milk into a cup and reached for the teapot. "How was he when he came in last night?"

Maria stood up and straightened the cloth. "Drunk."

That explains the noise. "Have the boys gone to school already?"

"No, they're not down yet. They won't have time for breakfast at this rate." Maria strode to the bottom of the stairs. "What are you two doing?"

"Coming." A second later, Billy jumped down the last couple of steps with Vernon chasing him.

"Vernon, be careful; you nearly knocked me over." Rebecca followed them to the table, with Alice close behind. "You wouldn't run like that if your dad was here."

"We heard him go out." Vernon grinned at Billy, but Maria swung a hand at the top of his head.

"We'll have less of that. If you two had been better behaved last night, he wouldn't have been so upset."

"We were only laughing." Vernon took a piece of bread and butter and stuffed it in his mouth.

Billy nodded. "It's not our fault he was in such a foul mood. It was James."

Rebecca settled Alice in her seat and took her own chair. "He's right." She stared at Maria. "Why did you tell George about his job offer? You knew he'd be angry, which is why we agreed to say nothing."

"Don't go blaming me." Maria's face reddened. "George was bound to find out sooner or later, and it was better for me to tell him than for him to find out from someone else."

Nell's eyes flicked between Rebecca and Maria, but she bit her tongue. She didn't want to get involved.

"You could have fooled me." Rebecca filled her own teacup. "Anyway, where is he?"

"Who?" Maria's tone was sharp.

"James. I know George has gone out; he woke the whole house this morning with the noise he made."

Maria looked at Billy. "Was James out of bed?"

Billy nudged his brother. "We'd better go; we'll be late for school."

Vernon didn't need to be told twice, and within seconds the two of them disappeared through the front door.

"What's going on?" Maria turned to Nell. "Have you seen him?"

Nell shook her head. "I'll go and check the bedroom."

Without waiting for a reply, Nell slipped out from the

table and hurried upstairs. When she reached the landing, she peered into the front room. As usual, the double bed shared by the younger boys was a mound of blankets, but she walked into the room to see James' bed was still pristine. *He mustn't have come home last night.*

Her heart sank. Where could he have stayed? She leaned on the door frame while she prepared to go back downstairs. *Maria will be furious.*

"What are you doing up there? Tell him to come down here."

Maria's face was peering up the stairs when Nell returned to the landing.

"He isn't here."

"Not here? What do you mean?"

Nell stepped aside as Maria pushed past and barged into the bedroom.

"He's stayed out all night?"

"It looks like it."

"I'll kill him." Maria charged down the stairs. "Wait until George hears of this."

"No!" Nell's voice squeaked, and blood rushed to her cheeks as Maria stared at her.

"What did you say?"

"I said ... well ... I meant, the reason he might not have come home last night was because of the way George treated him. It wouldn't surprise me if he's too frightened. Telling George about this won't make things better."

"He had every right to be angry with him. Do you know how much trouble he went to getting that apprenticeship? Not to mention the considerable indenture he paid for the privilege. He won't sit by and watch James throw it all away because of some fancy idea about going to sea."

"No." Nell walked back down the stairs as Maria's eyes bored into her.

"You think we should let him do what he wants, don't you?"

"I ... well ... it would be nice if he had some say in the matter. Even if you sit and talk to him ... explain what you've just told me. He probably hasn't considered that."

"Nell's right." Rebecca held out a chair for Maria. "James will never be a match for George. He's still a young boy, and he's more sensitive. If George carries on speaking to him like that, he's going to frighten him away."

"Where would he go?" Maria crossed her arms over her chest. "None of the neighbours would take him in. Not without telling us."

"Maybe not, but he earns a wage now. I'm sure he could find a shared room somewhere..." Nell stopped. *Windsor Street?*

"What's up with you?"

"Nothing." Nell shook her head. "I ... erm ... it's just struck me that he might not come back and ... well, he could be anywhere. I'm sure none of us want that."

"He wouldn't dare. Not without a word of warning."

"He might." Nell once again gestured for Maria to take a seat. "Even if he doesn't go for good, he may not want to come home while George is here."

"You mean he'll wait until he goes back to sea?" Rebecca asked.

"Possibly. Or he may wait until he knows he's out. Like tonight when he's in the alehouse." Nell turned to Maria.

"The thing is, I don't think you should make things worse by mentioning any of this to George. He won't understand."

Maria finally sat down. "All right. I'll say nothing of it for now, but if he..."

"Maria, no." Nell put a hand on her sister's. "No threats. He had enough of them last night. I suspect all he wants right now is a friendly smile."

"Well, he won't get one from me, the trouble he's caused."

Nell shook her head. "You really do make things difficult for yourself. The way you're carrying on, you'll drive him away for good. Is that what you want?"

"No, of course not."

"You'd better sort yourself out then, or that's exactly what will happen."

CHAPTER 8

Nell fastened Alice's cloak and checked her hat was pulled down over her ears, before reaching for the basket.

"There we are. Shall we go shopping?"

Alice nodded. "I like shopping."

"I do, too. Let's see what they have today, shall we?" *And please God, let Jack be outside the alehouse.*

Nell's stomach fluttered as they walked to the end of Newton Street, but as she turned left into Windsor Street, her pace slowed. *He's not here.* She searched the length of the street. *What do I do now?*

She studied the row of terraced houses on her left. *I'm sure he lives in one of these.* But which one? She'd never been to his house, he'd always called for her, but he must have mentioned where he lived. *Why didn't I pay more attention?* Her pace quickened and she counted up the numbers as she walked past. One thirty-two. *Was that it? Possibly. I don't remember.* She paused and bit her lip, studying the houses on either side, before staring back at the door. *Do I knock? No. I'll get the shopping first.*

She hadn't reached the end of the terrace when a door slammed and footsteps sounded behind her. Increasing her stride, she glanced over her shoulder, but stopped when she saw Jack, his clothes dishevelled.

"What's the matter? Did you oversleep?"

He ran a hand through his hair. "Not exactly, but I didn't get much sleep last night."

Nell cocked her head to one side. "Why not?"

"I ... erm ... I had a visitor."

"Please say it was James. Is he all right?"

"He is now." Jack plunged his hands into his pockets. "He was waiting for me when I left the alehouse and told me he couldn't go home. Thankfully, one of the blokes sharing my room left yesterday morning and so I sneaked him in."

"Wasn't he worried his dad might see him?"

"Oh, he was worried all right, but he'd already seen him leave, so he knew he was safe." Jack held Nell's gaze. "He told me what happened last night."

Nell turned her back on Alice. "It was awful. George was close to taking his belt to him..."

"I heard. That's why I've offered to let him use my room for as long as there's a spare bed. It should give him three or four days, but he can probably stay for longer if he doesn't mind sleeping on the floor. He won't go home while his dad's there."

"I don't blame him."

"Where's James?" Alice peered around Nell's skirt and stared up at Jack. "Mam wants to see him."

Nell crouched down beside her. "We want to keep it a surprise at the moment; can you do that? Mam likes surprises."

Alice's nose wrinkled. "Is he hiding?"

"He's playing a game; hide and seek. He'll be home soon." Nell straightened up and turned back to Jack. "Has he gone to work?"

"He has. I persuaded him it was for the best because if he wants to leave home, he'll need money for rent."

"Do you think he'll take the job on the liner and disappear?" Nell's voice croaked at the thought of James being forced away.

Jack shrugged. "It's too early to tell. I told him its always easier to ask for forgiveness than permission, but I don't think he believes me."

"I hope he doesn't. You'll get him into all sorts of trouble."

"Well, if you can do better, you're welcome to call and see him later. There's a sitting room we're allowed to use, and it's never busy when the alehouse is open. I'll stand at the door and keep everyone out if you like."

Nell smiled. "Thank you. You've not lost your caring side."

"You don't have to be caring to want to stop someone getting a beating."

"No, I suppose not. I don't know when I'll be able to sneak out, though. I'll have to wait until George is in the alehouse and hope Maria puts Alice to bed. It's usually my job."

Jack gestured towards Alice, who was getting restless. "She won't say anything, will she?"

Nell shook her head. "I'll buy her some sweets and she'll forget about it soon enough."

"You'd better be right. I don't want James in any more trouble." Jack ran his eyes over Nell. "He speaks very highly of you. He told me you'd like to go to sea one day. You never mentioned it to me."

The comment caught Nell off guard, and she laughed. "Whether I'd like to or not is irrelevant. Glamorous ships are not for the likes of me."

Jack sighed. "Nor me. Not at the moment, anyway. I'm thinking of getting a land- based job."

Nell raised an eyebrow. "Around here?"

"Of course around here, where else would I go?" His face became serious. "Would you consider walking out with me again if I did?"

Nell's heart skipped a beat. "You mean you're thinking of giving up the sea for good?"

Jack nodded. "I'm not getting any younger and it's hard work on a sailing ship. What do you say, Nell?"

"Well, I don't know. What about your trip in March, will you cancel that?"

He shook his head. "I'm afraid I can't get out of it, but if I knew you'd be waiting for me when I get back, I wouldn't sign up for another one." There was a twinkle in his eye as he smirked at her. "Can we try again?"

Her heart pounded as his dark eyes pleaded with her. "As long as you promise this next trip will be the last."

A smile spread across his lips. "I promise. It's about time I settled down. Going to sea is a boy's job or one for officers. I don't want to be a second mate for the rest of my life."

"But that's an officer rank."

Jack snorted. "A junior one. I still get the jobs the captain and first mate don't want to do."

Nell couldn't keep the grin off her face. "What will you do around here then?"

"I've not thought about it yet. I may find something with the Mersey Docks and Harbour Board, or possibly the Customs House. I won't be doing manual work."

"Why not? I could ask Tom to find something where he works, if you like."

Jack shook his head. "I'd end up being a labourer, which would be even worse than being a second mate. No one will offer me an apprenticeship at my age."

Nell nodded. He may only be in his mid-twenties, but he was too old to learn a trade. "Let's hope you can find something with a desk then." Her eyes fluttered at him. "You might even earn more money doing that."

Jack walked her to the shop and she bid him farewell with a promise that she'd call to see James later that evening. She took Alice's hand as she watched him stroll to the alehouse.

"You've been a good girl, haven't you? Would you like some sweeties for keeping our secret?"

Alice nodded and once they were inside, she pointed at a jar of jelly beans.

"An ounce, please." Nell counted her money as the shopkeeper weighed out the sweets. *Thank goodness James won't be home for tea. I wouldn't have enough.*

. . .

Maria was scrubbing the scullery floor when Nell walked back into the living room.

"What kept you?" She tucked a loose strand of hair behind her ear. "You should have been back twenty minutes ago."

"I, erm..." *Let's get this over with.* "I met Jack."

Maria stopped what she was doing and joined her at the table. "You've been talking to him?"

"Why shouldn't I?" Nell hung up her cloak. "He said his next trip will be his last, and he's going to get a job around here."

Maria's eyes narrowed. "A likely tale. I hope he wasn't saying that to get you to walk out with him again."

"Why can't he change his mind?" Nell unbuttoned Alice's cloak.

"Nell! Have you forgotten what he did to you? A year ago he had a choice between going to sea and staying here with you, and we haven't seen him since. The sea's in his veins. Can't you see that? He'll no sooner give up sailing than George will."

"But he is. He's realised he'll never be a captain, so he might as well settle down."

"With you?" Maria's eyes were wide.

"Perhaps." Nell shrugged. "We didn't talk about that."

"But that's what you'd like, isn't it?" Maria shook her head. "Good grief, Nell, after all he's put you through. You should have more sense."

"Why shouldn't we settle down together if he gets a job here?"

"Because it won't last. You know as well as I do, he

wants to be a master mariner. He's not going to give that up for you."

"But he will. He's promised."

"Well, don't come crying to me when he feels the pull of the sea and you get left behind."

Nell stamped her foot on the stone floor. "Why can't you be happy for anyone? Jack and I want to spend time together, and Rebecca wants to be married, but you've done nothing but complain about both. It's not our fault George is like he is and you have to put up with him."

"That's enough, it's got nothing to do with George. I'm not happy about you seeing Jack again because it will bring nothing but trouble, and I don't want you getting hurt ... again."

"That's for me to decide." Nell flapped her arms by her sides. "I'm twenty-three. Most of my friends are already married and running their own houses." She stroked a hand across the top of Alice's head as she stood beside her. "Many have even got their own children."

"On your head be it, then. I want nothing to do with it."

Maria stopped as the back door opened and Rebecca joined them.

"And is that why you're being so hard on her, too, because you can see trouble ahead?" Nell pointed at her sister.

"What's going on?" A frown settled on Rebecca's face as her eyes flicked between Nell and Maria.

"She's seeing Jack again." Maria flounced back to the scullery. "You talk some sense into her."

"Even though he's going back to sea?" Rebecca's voice was quiet as she sidled over to Nell.

"He's doing one last trip and then he's promised to get a land-based job."

Rebecca smiled. "That's wonderful. It was worth waiting for him then."

"I hope so. What about you? How's she been?"

Rebecca glanced over her shoulder and pulled Nell closer to the window. "She's told me not to say a word to anyone about the marriage until Mr Grayson's talked to George. The poor man doesn't even know he has to until I speak to him tonight."

Nell rested a hand on her sister's. "Don't you worry; we'll find a way to make the arrangements, and she needn't know about it."

CHAPTER 9

Maria fussed with the table as if she were hosting an elaborate party, rather than preparing for a family meal. She'd been baking all afternoon and placed an impressive meat and potato pie in the centre.

"That smells nice." Nell positioned a plate of bread and butter alongside it.

"I hope so." Maria pushed the bread closer to the pie. "I've made a sandwich cake for later, too. George likes his cake." She ushered Alice to a seat at the far corner of the table. "You sit there and be quiet."

Rebecca came silently down the stairs and joined them. Her hair curled around her face, fresh from the rags that had bound it all afternoon.

"You look nice." Nell smiled at her. "I hope Mr Grayson appreciates all this effort you go to."

"He does, but I wanted to make an extra effort tonight. I need to speak to him about George." Rebecca's mouth twisted as Nell stared down at her everyday grey dress.

"I said I'd meet Jack later, but he'll have to take me as he finds me. I don't have time to make myself as glamorous as you..."

Maria cut Nell short and dived towards the front door as George walked past the window. "Sit down, both of you, he's here." She reached for the handle and opened the door with a smile. "You're here. Have you had a nice day?" She ushered him into the room. "Would you like a cup of tea before we sit at the table?"

"No, I'm starving." He paced across the room. "Where is everyone?"

"Billy and Vernon are washing their hands. I'll go and get them." Maria rushed up the stairs, leaving Nell and Rebecca with George.

"Where's James?"

"I, erm, I've not seen him." Nell glanced to Rebecca, but she was more concerned with the neckline of her dress. "I'm sure we can start without him, though."

"Is he always late?" George reached for the bread.

"No, not usually, but ... but sometimes he's delayed..." Nell fidgeted with her fingers. "If there's extra work." She exhaled as Maria returned with Billy and Vernon.

"You two sit down and behave." Maria smiled at George. "Everything's ready. Just let me get the teapot."

"No, let me. You serve the pie." Nell carried the kettle to the scullery but found herself in no hurry to make the tea. By the time she returned and took the seat next to Alice, a slice of pie was in her place. "That looks nice."

"I was talking to Jack Riley this afternoon."

Nell knew George was speaking to her, even though he didn't take his eyes from his plate.

"He told me you're walking out together again."

"Yes." Nell coughed to clear the squeak from her throat. "I met him this morning, and he said he's giving up going to sea after his next trip."

"He told me that too, although why he'd do that, I've no idea."

"He said he's tired of only being a second mate."

"There's no reason he can't become a first mate. I told him to take his exams, anyway. He'll be glad of them one day."

Maria put a hand on George's. "I don't think Nell wants him to go to sea if they're walking out together. If they ever get married, she'd like him at home. Like you were when we were first married."

George grunted. "They can still do that for a year or two, but when the time comes for him to sail again, at least he'll have the qualifications. It makes sense to me. And he'll earn more money, especially if he makes it to master mariner."

Nell's stomach churned. "He said he didn't want to do that any more."

George shook his head. "You mark my words, a man like Jack will never lose his love of the sea."

"Oh." Nell flicked a piece of pie around her plate.

"I wouldn't worry though." George held his plate out for more pie. "By the time he goes back, you'll have your hands full with the kiddies. As long as he leaves you with enough money, you'll hardly miss him."

"I think there's more to it than that." Maria tittered. "I miss you when you're not here."

George grunted. "Only because you spend the money faster than I can earn it. At least you have James' wage now." He paused at mention of his son's name. "Where's he got to?"

Maria stared at the unoccupied place as if she'd only just noticed it.

"Actually, I've remembered..." Nell gulped as all eyes turned to her. "He said he was meeting a friend after work. I expect he'll be back later."

"What friend?" Maria's brow furrowed. "He's never usually late."

"I, erm ... I don't remember him mentioning a name."

"Well, if he knows what's good for him, he'd better be back by the time I get home." George cut another slice of pie. "I won't have him upsetting his mam like this."

Maria nodded and wiped a finger under her eyes. "He left without a word."

She hadn't even noticed! Nell shuddered under George's glare. "He hasn't left..."

"You're his mouthpiece, are you?"

"No, not at all, but he was upset..."

"I'll give him upset. How do you think I feel having a son who wants to be a *steward*?"

"It must be a respectable job." Rebecca took the slice of sandwich cake Maria handed to her. "Mr Grayson says many young men would like to work on the transatlantic ships."

"They're all welcome to it, as long as they're not my sons." He glared at Billy and Vernon. "Are you two listening?"

They both nodded before Vernon found his voice.

"I want to build ships."

George stood up. "I should hope so. Right, I'll see you all later."

There was a collective sigh of relief as George pulled the door closed behind him.

"That went better than last night." Maria smiled to herself as she poured another cup of tea. "Perhaps I'll make another pie tomorrow."

"It was because James wasn't here." Billy's words echoed Nell's thoughts.

"Nonsense. He wanted to know where he was."

Billy rolled his eyes. "Only so he could have another go at him."

"Exactly. How can you not see that?" Rebecca stood up and reached for her cloak. "Right, I need to leave; I'll see you later."

"I'll come with you." Nell nearly tripped over the leg of the chair in her haste to leave the table. "Let me get my hat and cloak."

"Where are you going?" Maria stopped before she could cut the boys more cake.

"I ... erm ... I said I'd meet Jack."

"What about the tidying up?" A scowl returned to Maria's face.

"Would you mind doing it on your own? Please. Just this once." Nell fastened the buttons around her neck. "I'll make up for it tomorrow." Without giving her time to respond, Nell dashed through the front door and waited for Rebecca to follow her.

"That was close." She pulled her hat over her ears.

"Where are you meeting Jack?" Rebecca glanced up and down the street.

"Erm, on Windsor Street."

"Isn't he walking around to meet you? Mr Grayson wouldn't let me walk out on my own. He's waiting for me." She waved to a tall man in a bowler hat on the opposite side of the street.

"When we arranged to meet, I wasn't sure if I'd have told Maria, so I didn't want to risk her finding out before I was ready. Why doesn't Mr Grayson ever knock on the door? We hardly know him."

Rebecca rolled her eyes. "For similar reasons to you, probably. You know what Maria's like; I don't want to give her an excuse not to like him."

"In the way she doesn't like Jack." Nell groaned. "At least Mr Grayson has the chance to make a good impression; Jack's already been judged and found wanting. Even George doesn't believe he'll give up the sea."

"Not walking around to meet you doesn't help."

"Don't blame him. I thought it was safe enough for me to walk around the corner."

"He should have talked some sense into you. You must let us escort you."

"There's no need; it's not far." Nell turned to leave, but spotted Mr Grayson walking towards them.

"Honestly, it's no trouble. He's here now." Rebecca's face lit up as he approached.

"Good evening, ladies." His eyes glistened as he put an arm around Rebecca's shoulders. "Is there a problem?"

"No, not at all. You remember Nell, don't you? She's walking out with someone, but he's not here to meet her, and she wants to walk by herself."

"You can't do that." A shadow crossed Mr Grayson's face. "He should be here to meet you."

"He wanted to … but there are reasons why he couldn't. He only lives around the corner. I can make my own way there…"

Mr Grayson studied the thick grey clouds. "Nonsense, the night's far too dark for a young lady to be walking on her own. I wouldn't dream of letting Rebecca walk out without me."

Rebecca nestled into his chest. "He's such a gentleman."

"Only for you, my dear." He offered Rebecca his arm as he turned to Nell. "We'll walk with you."

"As long as you're sure." Nell hesitated, but fell into line beside Rebecca; not that her sister noticed, given the way she gazed into Mr Grayson's eyes.

"Where will you walk once you've dropped me off?" Nell asked.

Rebecca giggled. "Only down to the river. It's quiet once all the workers have gone home."

Nell wasn't sure why Rebecca was laughing, but shrugged as they drew level with Jack's house.

"Right, we're here now." Nell stopped outside the three-storey building. "Have a nice evening."

"We're not leaving you on your own." Mr Grayson stepped towards the house. "I insist on knocking on the door for you."

"No, honestly. I can do it." Nell moved sideways to block his way.

"You can't go into a strange house by yourself." The sparkle on Rebecca's face disappeared.

"I'm not going in, just letting him know I'm here."

"Well, we'll wait until Jack's ready to walk out with you."

Nell took a deep breath. "Rebecca, this is Jack we're talking about, not some stranger. I'll be perfectly safe."

"If he didn't come to pick you up, how do you know he's even home?"

"That's right." Mr Grayson squeezed past Nell and banged on the front door. "We can't leave you on your own."

Nell's heart pounded as she stood beside Mr Grayson. *Please God, don't let James answer.* After a second knock, the door opened and Jack stood on the threshold staring at them.

"Nell?" His eyes flicked to Mr Grayson. "What's going on?"

"Is this him?" Mr Grayson stared down at Nell. "He's not even got his coat on. Are you sure he knew you were coming?"

"Yes, he did, but ... I'm a little earlier than we arranged." She smiled at Jack, whose face had frozen as he watched the exchange. "You remember Rebecca, don't you? This is Mr Grayson, her betrothed. He and Rebecca walked me here."

Jack snapped out of his trance and extended his hand. "It's nice to meet you. Thank you for that, I'm sure it's appreciated."

Mr Grayson shook his hand. "We're heading to the river, so it was no trouble, but I really must question your judgement on letting her walk out on her own."

"And I'm grateful for your concern, but I'm sure she'd have been fine."

Mr Grayson's nostrils flared. "You should never assume

that." He hesitated as if deciding whether to leave, but at Jack's silence he returned to Rebecca's side. "Right, well, I've said my piece. Good evening to you both."

Jack and Nell watched Mr Grayson take Rebecca's arm as they set off along the road.

"What was all that about?"

"I'm sorry. I made the mistake of leaving the house with Rebecca and they insisted on walking me round." She scanned the street. "Is James still here?"

Jack nodded. "He's in the living room. Come in quickly."

Relief crossed James' face as Nell walked in. "Aunty Nell, thank you for coming. You've not told anyone I'm here, have you?"

"No, I managed to keep it a secret." The room was unwelcoming with only thin curtains at the window and minimal ornaments on the mantelpiece. Nell pulled her cloak more tightly around her as she perched on the settee beside him.

"Let me put more coal on the fire." Jack knelt by the hearth. "Mrs D doesn't like us putting too much on in case we all go out."

Nell turned to James as Jack tended the flames. "You must come home. Your dad's been asking after you."

"What did you say?"

"I told him you were meeting a friend after work. I'm not sure he believed me, though."

James ran a hand through his hair. "Was he mad?"

Nell shook her head. "He wasn't as bad as he was last night. I think perhaps he was tired when you saw him."

James grimaced. "You're too kind to him; that wasn't

68

down to tiredness. The way I feel, it wouldn't bother me if I never saw him again."

Nell took hold of his hand. "You don't mean that. Can't you pretend you're enjoying work while he's here? It won't be for long and it will make life easier."

"It's easy for you to say."

"Maybe, but I'm sure you can do it. Will you come home with me tonight? The longer you stay away, the harder it will be."

James looked to Jack. "Will that spoil your evening?"

"That depends." Jack wandered to the chair opposite Nell and held her gaze. "Are you happy for James to go home before you?"

The smile slipped from Nell's lips as her eyes widened. "I can't stay here on my own."

"I don't expect you to, we can take a walk now we're walking out together."

Nell relaxed. "Yes, I'm sorry, I wasn't thinking. Things have been strange over these last few days."

"Not as strange as the idea that Jack could end up being my uncle." James grinned, causing Nell's cheeks to flush.

"It's far too soon to say that. We've only just got back together again..."

"But it's not as if you haven't known each other for years." James winked at Jack. "For what it's worth, if you propose marriage to her, I'll be thrilled."

CHAPTER 10

Jack cut a slice of cheese off the block in the middle of the table and arranged it on top of his bread and butter. Despite being home for over six weeks, it was still a treat to eat fresh food. The salted meat and dry biscuits were things he wouldn't miss when he left the merchant navy.

He sat at the table with two fellow lodgers, but nobody spoke. Each was engrossed in their food, and Jack smiled at the images running through his mind. He'd forgotten how much he'd missed Nell, but he now knew he was making the right decision. One last trip and he could spend the rest of his life with her.

Mrs Duffy disturbed him as she placed a fresh pot of tea on the table. "Have you finished with that?" She nodded towards the cheese.

"Why don't we save you the job of putting it away?" Jack smirked as each man reached for another slice. "We can finish it."

"I'll be putting up the rent if you carry on like this;

you're eating me out of house and home."

"Don't worry, you won't have me here for much longer." Jack took a bite of the cheese. "By this time next week..."

"I know, you're off on your travels again. I don't suppose your young lady's very pleased about you going."

Jack's smile dropped. "She understands." He glanced at the clock on the mantelpiece. "In fact, I'd better be going. I said I'd pick her up at six so we can walk while it's still light. I'll see you later."

Jack fastened the buttons of his coat as he trotted to the corner of Newton Street. His pace slowed as he caught his breath and spotted Nell waiting for him in the living room window. No sooner had she seen him than she disappeared, only to open the front door and close it quickly behind her.

"What's the matter?"

"Nothing, I'm just pleased to see you." She smiled up at him as he offered her his arm.

"I thought you were always pleased. What's special about tonight?"

"Nothing ... except George is out, so we didn't have to wait for him to leave the table."

A frown crossed Jack's face. "He was in the alehouse earlier, but he didn't say he was doing anything. What's he up to?"

Nell shrugged. "I neither know nor care. It's the first time I've seen James smile for weeks."

The wind was brisk as Jack led them along Upper Parliament Street towards the river. "How's he doing? I've not seen much of him since he left Windsor Street."

"He'll survive. He's been going into Liverpool while

George is around. As soon as the coast is clear, I'm sure he'll be back and you can have a pint together."

A frown creased Jack's brow. *But I'll be gone by then. Has she forgotten?* He gazed out over the river. *I'm not reminding her now.*

As they reached the dock road, he steered her to the left, away from the docks. The river was slightly more picturesque in that direction.

"Have you done anything about finding a job yet?" Her voice was soft compared to the shouts he'd grown accustomed to on the ship.

"It's too early yet."

"But you could make some enquiries." She smiled up at him. "It would be nice if you had something to come back to. Your money won't last long."

Jack's heart skipped a beat as he turned away. *Oh Lord. I didn't tell her how long I'm going for. How did I forget?* An inner voice hollered in his head. *You didn't forget. She didn't ask, and you were too much of a coward to tell her.* The colour drained from his face as Nell continued to gaze up at him.

"What's the matter? You've gone very pale."

"I'm fine, it's just that..." He took a deep breath. "I don't think I told you how long I'll be away on this trip."

"I assumed you'd be back by the summer."

"Ah." Jack paused as he ushered her across the road. "Actually, it will be longer than that. Probably most of the year."

"How much of the year?" Her smile disappeared.

"I can't say exactly, but it may well be autumn by the time I'm back." *If I'm lucky.*

Nell's eyes were wide. "But that's months off. The way you were talking, I'd hoped you'd be on a shorter trip, seeing the last one was so long."

Jack ran a finger down her cheek. "I didn't do it on purpose. When I arranged it, I'd no idea we'd be walking out together by the time I went back."

"No, I don't suppose you did."

"But let's look on the bright side. These long voyages pay well, and it will set us up for when we get..." He paused.

"For when we get what?" Her eyes filled with tears as she gazed up at him.

"For when we're together again. We'll be able to see more of each other and..."

"And?"

"And we'll see. You will wait for me, won't you?"

"Of course I will. Why wouldn't I?"

"Because you're a beautiful woman, and I worry that once I'm away someone else may take their chance with you."

Nell's cheeks flushed. "They haven't so far, but even if they did, I wouldn't be interested." She hesitated as her eyes searched his. "I love you, Jack." She let his hands caress her cheeks.

"And I love you. Why else do you think I'm giving up the sea? It's not a decision I've taken lightly."

Her smile returned. "So you'd do another voyage if it wasn't for me?"

"If you'd turned me down, I'd have gone off to mend my broken heart."

"Really?"

His smile was tender as he bent forward and kissed her on the lips. "I'd have no reason to stay if you weren't waiting for me."

Nell put a hand to her chest. "I don't know what to say."

He pulled her into the shelter of a doorway and wrapped his arms around her. "Then don't say anything."

Nell thought her heart would burst. Perhaps this was what Rebecca had meant all those weeks ago. Why had it taken her so long to tell Jack she loved him? If she'd told him earlier, she may have felt his embrace sooner. And his lips. Now, with only a week left, she'd have to make the most of him.

As the clock on a local church struck half past nine, they disentangled themselves and put their heads into the wind as they walked back along the dock road. Neither spoke until they reached Parliament Street and the buildings on either side of the road shielded them from the worst of the weather.

"That's better." Nell smiled up at him. "I love the river. It's just a shame the wind does too."

Jack laughed. "And I'm very glad it does. My sailing ship wouldn't get very far if it didn't."

"I don't suppose it would, but that means I should pray for wind more often because it will bring you back to me sooner."

He wrapped an arm around her shoulders. "If only it were that simple."

"I don't know what I'll do while you're away. I've got so

used to seeing you of an evening, it will be dreary sitting with Maria again, with nothing to entertain me but my knitting."

Jack squeezed her. "I'll write as often as I can, although the first stop won't be until we reach South Africa. Once we get to the coast of China, we'll have more stops, so I'll send a letter from each port."

"It will take you such a long time to get there, though." She rested her head on his shoulder. "I wish I could go with you. I'd love to visit such exotic countries."

Jack kissed the top of her head. "I'll try to describe each place as best I can, but the docks of any town are not the most attractive feature. You might not be very impressed."

"I don't mind; being able to imagine all the things you see will be better than nothing."

"You'll have Rebecca's wedding to look forward to while I'm away."

Nell nodded. "I will. And I'll have plenty of time to help her arrange everything. They've set a date for June."

"Mr Grayson finally asked George, did he?"

"He did. Rebecca said he'd been talking to him in the alehouse for a few nights to get to know him better and was waiting to catch him in a good mood. That's why it took him so long. Anyway, George was pleased to be asked, although he said he wouldn't be at the wedding with it being so soon." Nell smiled. "He even offered to pay, as long as they don't invite too many guests."

"Good old George." Jack chuckled. "I've not had any problem with him myself, maybe because he's at his happiest in the alehouse. I expect he'll be glad to see the back of me, though. It'll be one less guest to invite."

"Well, I'm not. Imagine, going to a marriage service alone."

"I've never thought about it, but you'll have James to go with."

"I'm sure he'll be delighted to be lumbered with his old aunt."

Jack rolled his eyes. "I'd hardly call you that. You're only seven years older than him."

"You know what I mean. Perhaps I should tell him to drop the 'Aunty' so it doesn't sound so strange." Nell's shoulders dropped as they approached the corner of Windsor Street. "Does this road get shorter each evening? It seems to take us no time to walk here."

"Perhaps we could stay at the docks for longer, then?"

Nell smiled. "I wish we could. What time is it?"

Jack put a hand through a gap in his coat to pull out his pocket watch. "Ten to ten."

"I suppose I've not much time to spare."

"Five minutes?" Jack raised an eyebrow, and she let him manoeuvre her towards the wall of the corner house.

"Will I see you tomorrow?"

"I hope so." He planted a kiss on the end of her nose. "Shall I pick you up at six o'clock?"

Nell nodded. "With any luck George will be out again, but if I'm late, it will be because he's at home."

Jack winked at her. "Leave George to me. I'll nip back to the alehouse once I've walked you home and have a word with him. He knows I go away again next week. I'll tell him to hurry up."

Nell laughed. "The best of luck with that then."

CHAPTER 11

Nell sat at the dining table, ignoring the bread and cold meat on her plate.

"Don't you want that?" Billy reached across to take the slice of boiled ham, but Nell offered him the whole plate.

"No, here, you have it."

"What's up with you?" Maria topped up her cup of tea. "Moping around won't do any good."

"You don't understand." Nell crossed her arms on the table.

Maria planted her hands on her hips. "If this is about Jack going to sea, of course I understand. How many times do you think I've been through this with George?"

A smile suddenly brightened George's face. "She knows I'll always come home."

"And I'm sure Jack will too, but I'm going to miss him so much." She looked up as Vernon sniggered from across the table. "You wait until you're older; you won't laugh then." She was in no mood to be civil.

"The time will fly by, you'll see, and when he comes back..."

Nell did a double take as George winked at her. *Has he been drinking? Maybe I should make the most of it.* She pushed herself up from her seat. "Will you excuse me? Jack will be here in five minutes and I need to fix my hat."

She hadn't finished fastening her cloak when a knock on the front door caused her to freeze. *Is that Jack? Why's he knocking?*

"Aren't you going to open it?" George turned to stare at her.

"Yes, of course." She pulled on the handle to find Jack standing on the footpath, his usual charming smile brightening his face. Not that it settled the churning in her stomach. "Is everything all right?"

"I wanted to say farewell to everyone. May I come in?"

Nell's eyes were wide as she held open the door. "We're just finishing tea."

"Jack!" George was on his feet before Jack could take off his cap.

"I've called to say cheerio. I need to be on the ship for seven o'clock tomorrow morning, so I don't suppose I'll be in the alehouse later. Unless something goes wrong."

George shook his hand. "You've nothing to worry about, you mark my words. Now, be off with you and put a smile on her face." He nodded at Nell.

"Yes, sir ... and thank you."

Maria sat tight-lipped as Jack bade farewell to the boys.

"God willing, I'll be back soon." He walked to Nell, who had stayed by the door, and ushered her outside. He was about to pull it closed behind them when James yanked it open and joined them on the street.

"Jack, don't go. I mean, not right at this moment."

"What's the matter?"

"Nothing. I just wanted to wish you a safe journey ... and to thank you for everything. I'll be sorry to see you go."

Jack slapped James on the back. "You take care of yourself and don't let your dad upset you. I've had a word with him, so he should be more understanding."

James' eyes widened. "Really! Oh, thank you."

Jack laughed. "I still wouldn't expect too much from him if you mention the stewarding again, but if you can keep your mouth shut, he should give you an easier time."

"I'll try to." James smirked as he turned to go into the house.

"Oh, and James."

James turned expectantly. "Yes?"

"Take care of your Aunty Nell for me."

"Don't worry, I will." James grinned at the two of them as he disappeared through the front door.

"Thank you for speaking to George. He won't listen to any of us." Nell allowed Jack to lead her along the road. "What did you say to him?"

"Nothing much."

"You must have said something. And why did you want to come inside?"

Jack shrugged. "We've been getting along rather well in the alehouse, and it seemed rude not to say goodbye. It could be years before we come across each other again. I hadn't seen James for a while either and I wanted to make sure he was all right."

Nell's shoulders relaxed. "You're so good. I don't know what you said to George, but he was like a different man tonight. I think it even surprised Maria."

"She wasn't pleased to see me, though."

"You noticed? I'm sorry…"

"It's not your fault, but what have I done to upset her?"

Nell sighed. "She doesn't believe you'll give up the sea."

"I'll prove her wrong then."

"George doesn't believe you either." Nell bit her lip as Jack gazed down at her. "He reckons that if we ever have a family, you'll be off again."

Jack put an arm around her shoulders. "He's assuming I'm the same as him, which, in case you haven't noticed, I'm not."

Nell grinned. "I had noticed, thankfully. Does that mean you'll stay with me once you come home?"

"I said I would." Jack gazed down the street towards the river. "Where was Rebecca tonight? I expected her to be at the table."

"She was, but she'd nipped upstairs to get herself ready for Mr Grayson. I must admit, she puts a lot of effort in for him. Not like me." Nell glanced down at her grey skirt. "I'll have to ask her to give me some advice while you're away."

Jack smiled at her. "Don't you do anything of the sort. You're perfect the way you are."

Nell was glad of the fading light as her cheeks flushed and she nestled against his arm. "And so are you. It's just a shame I'll be without you for so long. Are you all packed?"

"I am, not that I've much to take. Mrs D did my ironing for me. For an extra shilling, mind you."

"She knows how to make money, I'll say that for her, but you should have asked me; I'd have done it for you."

"I wouldn't dream of it. You've enough to do." He held her close. "How are you feeling?"

Nell squeezed her eyes tightly shut to hide her tears. "I'm fine. I keep telling myself that by this time tomorrow, it will be one day closer to you coming home."

"That's the way to look at it. It won't be easy for me, either, you know. Being stuck on a boat with forty other men, not to mention being battered by the high winds in those southern oceans."

"So why do you keep going back? I've heard of many men who give up after their first voyage."

"And I was nearly one of them. If I'm honest, I only went the second time because I had nowhere else to go. I was away for about a year and a half on that trip, and after that, it got easier."

"Don't you ever see your brothers or sister?"

He shook his head. "Not really, I visited my sister last year, but they all live too far away. They'd probably put up with me if I was desperate, but I'd rather not move away from here."

Nell snuggled into his arm as they reached the dock road and headed for the building opposite. "It's chilly out here tonight."

"I was thinking the same thing. Let's see if we can find somewhere a little warmer." He winked at her as he guided her across the road. "Somewhere nice and sheltered."

. . .

A tear ran down Nell's cheek as the church bells once again sounded for half past nine. Despite the shelter of the doorway, her feet were freezing, but she wanted tonight to last forever. She pulled herself closer to Jack and let him wrap his arms more tightly around her. How long would she have to wait to feel his touch again?

"Do you have to go?" She couldn't hide the squeak in her voice.

"You know I do." He kissed the top of her head as it rested beneath his chin. "I wish I'd known what I was doing when I signed up. The only thing I was interested in at the time was the money, but I promise, this will be the last voyage."

"You won't forget me, will you?"

"Of course not; I'm more worried you won't be here for me when I get back."

"You know I will." She wiped her cheeks on the front of his coat.

"I'd like to be sure."

"What do you mean?" Nell lifted her face to his, but he released her and put a hand in his pocket, retrieving a small package. He opened it carefully and laid a gold band studded with tiny diamonds on his hand. "Will you marry me, Nell? When I get back."

Nell's mouth dropped open.

"I've already asked George, in case you're worried."

"So that's why he was being so nice." A smile split her face. "Of course I'll marry you." She watched as he slid the ring onto her third finger. "It's beautiful."

Jack raised her hand to kiss the ring. "I hope you'll think of me every time you see it."

"How could I not?" She ran the index finger of her other hand over it. "I'll treasure it." She reached up to kiss him and he once again took her in his arms.

"This can be our place and our night. I love you, Nell. Please don't forget about me."

CHAPTER 12

George was already at the breakfast table the following morning when Nell arrived downstairs with Alice. She helped her into a chair and sat opposite Billy and Vernon. George nodded at her hand.

"You said yes, then?"

"She did." Maria's tone was brusque as she bustled into the room with the teapot.

George grabbed hold of Maria's wrist. "What's wrong with you? Jack's a good man, she could do a lot worse."

Nell gave him a weak smile. "Thank you for agreeing to it. It means a lot."

"The least I could do, especially now Rebecca's engaged, too." He smiled to himself. "By this time next year, I'll only have Alice to sort out."

"It's a good job you've a few years to save up for her." Maria plonked herself on her chair.

"What's going on here?" Rebecca swung herself around the bannister at the bottom of the stairs.

"Mam's not happy about Aunty Nell getting married." James kept his head down as he spoke.

"Why should she be any happier about her than she is of me?" Rebecca glared at her sister, but Maria focussed on her bread. "I don't remember Mam and Dad being so upset when you got married."

"You were too young to notice anything."

"That's enough." The familiar anger returned to George's eyes as he glared at them, but they suddenly softened. "I seem to remember they liked me well enough. They had no reason not to."

"Of course they didn't. You've been a good husband." Maria patted George on the hand as her eyes flicked between Rebecca and Nell. "You two should be thankful for everything he's done for you ... and that he's agreed to your weddings. They'll set us back a bob or two."

"I'm sure we are." Nell put her knife onto the table. "Excuse me, I need to go." She grabbed her hat and coat, but left the house carrying both. She didn't stop until she'd turned the corner onto Windsor Street. *What's got into Maria?*

She leaned against the wall to catch her breath, but the chill wind being tunnelled along the street hurried her into draping the cloak around her shoulders while she pulled on her hat. Once it was straight, she fastened her cloak and leaned back once more, feeling the new ring on her finger. She'd no idea where she was going, but wherever it was, at least she'd be alone. Tears welled in her eyes. Jack wouldn't have even left the Mersey but Maria had started already. *How will I manage for the next six months without him?*

She began walking along Windsor Street but stopped when she reached number one thirty-two. How long would it take for her to feel whole again? She lingered outside the house but turned around when she heard footsteps approaching.

"James."

"I had a feeling I'd find you here."

Nell gestured to the house. "I was passing..."

"I imagine it will get easier. It always does for Mam."

She nodded. "Maybe that's why she's cross with me, because she knows how hard it is."

James glanced around as Nell wiped the tears from her cheeks.

"I'm sorry. Give me a few days and I'm sure I'll be fine."

"Where are you going?" He indicated along the road.

"Nowhere in particular."

"Walk with me then." James held out his arm. "We need to get a move on though. I'm running late for work but hopefully you can keep up."

Nell chuckled. "I'll try." She kept in step with him as they headed down the hill towards the river, but by the time they reached the dock road, she was out of breath. "I'd better let you go. Perhaps we could take a more leisurely stroll this evening."

James smiled at her. "I'd like that. I'll see you later."

Nell stood on the corner and watched him head into the chaos that was the early morning trade. *I wonder where Jack's boat is.* She shook her head. *There's no point looking for it, I'll only upset myself again.* After pausing to get her bearings, she turned and headed away from the crowds, wandering without purpose until she reached the end of the Brunswick Dock. Less than twelve hours earlier she'd been here with Jack, but now look at it. There were men everywhere. With a sob, she carried on walking, staring out over the river. She wouldn't be visiting their special place for the foreseeable future.

Maria was setting the table for dinner by the time Nell arrived home.

"You've come back, then."

Nell hung her cloak on the hook. "I can easily go again if you're going to be like that."

Maria sighed. "I'm sorry, come and sit down. I've been on edge over the last few weeks."

"But why? You should be happy George is here."

"I am, when he's in a good mood, but it's always the same. Once he arrives, I worry about the day he'll leave again. I always know it's coming."

"But that must spoil the time he's home. Not that he spends much time here. He's either in town or in the alehouse. Have you spent more than a few hours on your own with him?"

Maria's shoulders slumped. "You're too young to understand, but life won't always be full of romance like it is now. When you get older, you spend your time keeping things going. I've learned that if I get too close to George, it's harder when he leaves again."

"Does he know this?"

Maria stood up and flicked her duster over the mantelpiece. "Don't be silly. He doesn't want to hear nonsense like that."

"Is that why you're so against Jack? Because you think

he'll go back to sea and I'll end up leading the same sort of life as you? Aren't you happy?"

Maria turned back to face her. "He's a second mate. The sea's in his blood, and knowing Jack, he'll have his eye on being a first mate and then a master mariner. I'm sorry, Nell, but whatever he's told you, I don't believe this will be his last voyage."

"But it will be; he promised..."

Maria threw her hands in the air. "Men have been making promises for centuries, and what good has it done us? None. Despite what he may have told you, he won't change."

Tears pricked Nell's eyes, and she reached for her handkerchief. "He will."

"Don't cry." Maria's tone softened. "I didn't mean to upset you, but I worry about you. It's not easy being a sailor's widow."

"There's no need to; we love each other..."

Maria closed her eyes as she shook her head. "Do you think George and I didn't when we were first married? Of course we did, but life changes."

"Well, I'm not changing anything. I'm marrying Jack as soon as he comes home, whether you like it or not. Why can't you accept that and be happy for me?"

"Because I saw what he did to you last time." Maria shook her head. "It took you months to get over him, and as soon as I thought you were ready to find someone else, back he came. I can't shake the feeling he'll do the same all over again, and when he does, it's me who'll have to pick up the pieces."

"You've got it wrong. He really does mean it this time."
Nell smiled. "Trust me."

Despite his young age, James towered over Nell as they
strolled along Windsor Street towards the new houses.

"Thank you for walking this way. It's still too painful to
go along Windsor Street."

"It makes no difference to me; besides, it's nice to see
what they're doing down here." He led her to the left, down a
road of new houses. "Merlin Street. That's a strange name."

"It might be, but look at these." Nell peered through the
window of a house at the end of a row. "They've got a front
room as well as one at the back. Your mam was talking about
moving before next winter. One of these would be lovely."

James cupped his hand to the glass as he peered in.
"Dad won't pay for this. Especially if he's not living here."

"That's what your mam said. There's no harm in asking,
though. He's in a better mood than he was when he first
came home."

"Not that much better. At least not with me." James
took a step back, causing Nell to turn to face him.

"I've not noticed; what's he said?"

James shook his head. "He's not said anything directly,
but he called to see my master a couple of weeks ago and
seems to have got him to do his dirty work."

"How do you know?"

"I saw Dad coming into work one night as I was leaving.
The night he wasn't home for tea. I don't know what he
said, but the boss has been making snide comments ever

since about me doing women's work and how I need to try harder."

Nell cocked her head to one side. "I thought Jack had sorted things out for you."

"I think Jack did too, but you can't stop Dad that easily."

"What will you do?" Nell accepted James' arm again as they began their walk home. "Have you been able to speak to anyone at the shipping line who offered you the job."

He nodded. "I called in last week and told them I couldn't start when they wanted me to."

Nell put a hand on his arm. "I'm sorry."

"It's not your fault. They said I was a strong candidate and so they'd hold the job open for the time being, in case I change my mind. If I go, it will be when Dad's away."

"You mean you'll go without telling him?" A shiver ran down Nell's spine at the thought of George when he found out.

"It won't be straight away, but I can't think how else to do it. I'll wait until him and Mam have forgotten about it and then sneak off."

Nell's heart sank. "Oh, James, don't do anything rash. You'll need to come home at some point."

"Well, hopefully they'll appreciate me by then, instead of treating me like a freak. If I can get on a ship travelling to Australia, I'll be gone for the best part of the year. If they're not pleased to see me when I get back, I'll have enough money to rent a room. Like Jack did."

"Did you speak to Jack about it?"

The corners of his lips curled up. "I did. He said that if Mam and Dad are still mad at me, I could spend my shore leave with the two of you once you're married. I hope you don't mind."

Nell grimaced. "I'm sure I'd be happy for you to stay, but I don't want to do anything that causes a rift between me and your mam."

"She'll only have herself to blame if it does. I hope she'll see sense though, once Dad's out the way. I've been thinking about it, and the chances of me and him having shore leave at the same time are very slim. It could be years before I see him again."

Nell took a deep breath. "I suppose so. Do you think your master will try to stop you though, based on what your dad said to him?"

James shrugged. "He won't know anything about it until I don't turn up for work. In fact, I don't plan on telling anyone when I'm going."

"Not even me?" Nell's smile dropped.

"Not even you ... and trust me, you'll thank me when the time comes."

CHAPTER 13

Three months later

T he sun streamed through the window as Rebecca
stood in front of the mirror in the front bedroom.

"It's not too plain, is it?" She peered over her shoulder to
where Nell was fussing with the bustle and train on her
wedding dress.

"Not at all; it's lovely. I love this shade of grey too. It's
almost silver in the sunlight."

Rebecca smiled. "That's why I chose it, although my
eyes are tired of looking at it after all the stitching."

"You've done a wonderful job, though." Nell stood up.
"Once you're settled into your new home, will you make
one for me?"

Rebecca laughed. "After all the effort I've put into it,
you can have this one if you like."

"Oh." Nell's face dropped. "I suppose I could, although
it might need taking out a little."

Rebecca giggled. "I'm only teasing. Of course I'll make

you one. I'll probably wear this for church every Sunday from now until it no longer fits me."

Nell's eyes sparkled. "That may not be long off if you're fortunate."

Rebecca clasped her hands in front of her chest. "Oh, Nell, I'm so excited. Imagine, by this time next year, I could be a mam."

"And I may be on my way to joining you ... if you promise to make me a dress."

Rebecca laughed. "I'm sure Jack would marry you in your working clothes if you had nothing else."

Nell smirked. "I hope so, but he feels so far away at the moment."

"Aren't you expecting him home next month?"

"No, the one after, but I've not heard from him for weeks, so I can't be certain. I hope the winds are strong enough to bring him back quickly."

Maria popped her head into the room. "What's going on in here? We need to leave for church shortly."

Nell moved out of the way as Rebecca turned to show Maria her dress.

"You've made a good job of it." She stepped forward to adjust the cape collar that covered her shoulders.

"Have you delivered Alice to Sarah?" Nell scowled and moved the collar back.

"I have. As soon as you came up here. How Sarah will manage with five of them, as well as that new baby, I don't know."

"She's used to it." Nell thought of her nieces and nephews. "Alice won't be any trouble compared to those boys."

"Maybe not, but you'd better get a move on. Tom will be here in a minute, not to mention the carriages."

Nell picked up the brush from the dressing table. "We won't be long, I only need to finish Rebecca's hair and put my dress on."

Rebecca perched on the end of one of the beds and helped Nell untie the rags that had been in her hair all night.

"These have worked well." Nell brushed the hair around her fingers as it fell into ringlets around Rebecca's face. "What did we do with those flowers?"

"There they are." Rebecca pointed to the bed and waited while Nell reached over for the small daisies and fastened them close to her hairline so they resembled a crown nestling in her dark hair.

"There we are; they look lovely."

Rebecca smiled at her reflection. "I hope Hugh thinks so."

Nell peered into the mirror over Rebecca's shoulder. "If he doesn't, he's a fool. Now, let me fix the veil."

She worked quickly with a handful of hairpins until it was secure. "They should hold it. Will you help me on with my dress?" She reached over to the bed on the opposite side of the room and held up the familiar emerald green dress she always wore for church. "Thank goodness this is still new enough to wear."

"You've no need to grumble, it's a lovely dress."

"I know, but I'll be positively dowdy compared to you."

"Nonsense." Rebecca lifted the dress for Nell to pull over her head, before she fastened the buttons up the back. "You look smashing."

"I will in a minute." She picked up the brush but stopped at the sound of a knock on the front door. "That will be Tom." She pulled the brush through her hair. "I won't be a minute. Let me twist this into my neck."

"Take your time. I'm sure an extra minute or two won't hurt."

Tom's deep voice reverberated around the living room by the time Nell led Rebecca onto the landing.

"Let me arrange the train so it follows you nicely down the stairs, then I'll go and announce your arrival." Nell grinned at her sister as she bent down to straighten the material. "This is so exciting. I can't wait for it to be me."

"Then why do I feel so nervous?" Rebecca put a hand to her chest. "It's only family downstairs."

"I'm sure I've no idea. Now, don't forget to smile."

Nell squeezed past her and hurried down the stairs with as much dignity as she could manage. Once in the middle of the room, she clapped to get everyone's attention. "Rebecca's ready."

She stepped out of the way as Tom walked to the foot of the stairs and offered a hand to Rebecca.

"My, you look lovely." He ran a hand over his slicked back hair as he gazed up at his sister, but Rebecca took an age to reach him, taking each step more slowly than the last. Everyone held their breath, until she reached for his hand and let him escort her to the centre of the room.

"Mr Grayson's a lucky man."

"I hope so. I like to think I'll make a good wife. He deserves it."

"And you deserve a husband to take care of you." He took her other hand and extended his arms to admire her dress. "As much as it's a shame George can't be here today, I'm honoured to be giving you away; I'll be the proudest man in the church."

"After Mr Grayson." James studied his aunt. "We can't deny that he's the fortunate one."

"He won't be if we don't get there soon." Maria marched towards the front door and beckoned to James, Billy and Vernon. "You three are in the front carriage with me and your Aunty Nell. Tom and Rebecca, you follow us in the second." She turned to Tom. "Give us five minutes to get there and take our seats before you leave. I'll let Mr Grayson know you're on your way."

An hour later, with a demure smile on her face, the new Mrs Grayson walked back down the aisle on the arm of her husband. The guests followed them outside and paused while Maria presented Rebecca with a horseshoe.

"Put it over the fireplace when you get home and it will bring you good luck." Maria stepped back and turned to the guests surrounding the couple. "Are we ready?"

To a chorus of cheers, handfuls of confetti appeared. Rebecca giggled and bowed her head as it rained down on them, but Mr Grayson brushed it from his shoulders.

"It's about time we were leaving."

"If you say so." Rebecca clung to his arm, bouncing on the balls of her feet as she turned to wave. "We'll see you at the house. Don't be long."

Nell stood with Maria as they watched Mr Grayson help Rebecca into the carriage. "That was lovely."

"It was nice enough; I hope they're happy together."

Maria's eyes narrowed as the carriage disappeared. "I don't know whether it's me, but Mr Grayson didn't seem as happy as I expected."

"He looked fine to me, it was probably nerves."

Maria nodded. "I suppose so. Hopefully, he'll have relaxed by the time we get back to the house. Speaking of which–" she turned to study the church clock "–we'd better get a move on, or we'll have a bunch of hungry people waiting for us."

Tom was waiting for them by the carriage when they arrived and a smile settled on his face as he took a seat.

"It's as well you told the boys to walk. It would have been a bit of a squeeze otherwise."

Maria settled back into the seat. "It will do them good."

"It went well, I thought." Nell smiled at her brother. "You made a good stand-in."

Tom laughed. "I did my best; it'll be you next. I don't suppose George will be home when you and Jack tie the knot, either. Have you got a date yet?"

"No, not yet. I had a letter a couple of weeks ago that he'd posted in South Africa. At the time, he said he was nearly halfway to China, and so based on the dates, I'm hoping he'll be home next month." Nell's smile broadened as Tom's faded.

"I wouldn't build your hopes up; I doubt he'll be home so quickly. Ships don't go all the way to the Far East only to turn around and come straight back again. What did he say exactly?"

"Not much, other than tell me about the scenery in Cape Town, but I thought..."

Tom shook his head. "I'd be surprised if they don't do

local voyages while they're over there, picking up goods and trading them again."

Maria scowled at him. "Don't say that to her."

"All right, let's work this out." Tom studied Nell. "When did he go? Early March?"

Nell nodded. "The sixth."

"So, if he left Liverpool on the sixth it would take about a month to get to Cape Town, which would fit with him posting the letter from South Africa in April. The thing is, South Africa's closer to Liverpool than it is to China, so we need to assume it will have taken at least six weeks to travel over there. That would take us to the end of May ... only a couple of weeks ago."

Nell wiped away a tear that threatened to fall. "But that's ten weeks."

"It is, but it means that even if they turned around and came straight back, he wouldn't be here before the end of August."

Nell's stomach churned as Tom's voice faded from her consciousness.

"As I said ... travel around the Far East for at least a month ... he's probably still in China."

Nell suddenly interrupted. "But they could be home by September?"

"I doubt..." Tom squirmed in his seat, and Nell turned to see Maria glaring at him. "Perhaps. Or maybe October."

"That's enough, Tom Parry. I'd like to see Nell with a smile on her face this afternoon." She patted Nell on the knee. "Take no notice of him. I'm sure Jack will be back soon enough."

CHAPTER 14

Nell rapped on the door knocker of Rebecca's new house and looked at Maria as she stepped back. "This is so exciting." She smiled down at Alice. "I hope she's ready for us."

"And I do." Alice bounced on the spot, but before her niece could clap her hands, Rebecca opened the door.

"Where've you been? I thought you'd never get here. Come on in. The tea's already brewing." Rebecca hugged Alice as she bounded into the house several paces ahead of Nell and Maria.

"It's lovely." Nell took in the newly papered walls. "It's about the same size as our house, but everything's so much newer."

"I know. I can't believe how fortunate Hugh was to find it, although I'm glad he did. I couldn't stay in his old lodgings a moment longer. Three weeks was quite enough, with his landlady interfering in *everything* we wanted to do. She wouldn't even let me cook for him."

"You seem to have settled in here, though." Maria made herself comfortable in an armchair by the fire.

"We have, but it's so quiet after living with you all these years. It's even quiet compared to being at Hugh's old place. There were always other men around there, but now it's just the two of us, it seems strange. I'm not used to it yet, especially at mealtimes. They've become very formal."

"I imagine they're a lot quicker, though. And quieter." Nell studied the fireplace. "Look at that range, so nice and shiny."

Rebecca stepped forward to show Nell the oven at the side of the fire. "I can do a whole batch of cakes and fit them all in at once."

"It's a wonder you have time." Maria leaned forward and peered into the oven. "You've the whole house to clean yourself."

"That's the thing, though." Rebecca picked up the teapot from the range and carried it to the table. "It doesn't take long at all. With there only being the two of us, it doesn't get nearly so untidy."

"That'll be because it's all new." Maria ran her hand over the top of the dresser.

"It could be that as well, but I'm not complaining." Rebecca poured the tea. "I could just do with more visitors in the afternoon to save me from being lonely."

"Well, you know where we are if you ever want company," Maria said.

"We've missed you." Alice smiled at her aunty as she sat on the rug in front of the fire.

"Ah, that's sweet. I've missed you, too."

"So why don't you ever call? I thought we'd see you most days." Nell passed a cup of tea to Maria.

"I-I don't know. I'm still finding my feet here, I suppose." Rebecca offered Maria a cake before she sat down and handed one to Alice.

"But you must be settled if you're worried about being lonely."

"I suppose..."

Nell had a glint in her eye as she took a seat next to Rebecca. "If you've time on your hands, will you make a start on my wedding dress?"

Rebecca's face lit up. "Have you heard from Jack?"

"No ... but I'm sure I will this week."

"You don't know that." Maria rolled her eyes at Rebecca. "I've tried to tell her, but she won't listen."

"You don't know he won't, you're just being mean."

"I'm not, I'm being realistic; you've not heard from him for months. I've had two letters from George."

"Which is all the more reason to expect something this week. It takes months for a letter to come all the way from China."

"It's not a competition." Rebecca helped herself to another cake. "I'm sure they both write when they can."

"You're right." Nell grinned at Rebecca. "So, what about my dress? I saw the material I'd like at the market in Liverpool last week."

"You went without me?" Rebecca pouted. "Why didn't you tell me you were going?"

"I'm sorry, but we thought you'd be busy ... with moving house and everything. We can go again whenever you like. I need your opinion on what to buy, anyway."

"I suppose I was busy." Rebecca bit down on her lip. "I should be able to go next week, though; I'll check with Hugh and let you know."

"There won't be a problem, will there?"

"No, of course not." Rebecca's voice squeaked. "But he likes to know what I'm doing and that I won't be on my own. I'll need some money from him, too."

Nell raised an eyebrow at Maria. "We've been on our own for so long, we don't think of these things. You can make the dress at our house, though, if you want an excuse to call." Nell grinned at her sister, but Rebecca shook her head.

"I'm better doing it here. There's more room for one thing and no chance of Vernon getting his grubby hands on it. Besides, I can work on it of an evening if it's here."

"That makes sense, although I had hoped to watch you make it." Nell's smile faded. "Does Mr Grayson keep you company after tea?"

"He sits with me for a while, but he'll nip to the alehouse at about nine o'clock. Only for an hour or so. He likes to keep in touch with what's going on, and I'm usually ready for bed by then, so I don't mind."

Maria sighed. "I wish George was as considerate, although I suppose he was when we were first married."

"They need to get out and mix. They don't get the chance during the day, like we do." Rebecca stood up to collect the dishes.

"I wish Jack was here; even if he was still living in Windsor Street." Nell handed Rebecca her cup. "I keep praying that a letter will arrive telling me he's on his way home. I'm so excited to see him, I can hardly wait."

"Well, make the most of it." Rebecca turned her back on them as she disappeared into the scullery.

"What do you mean?" Nell glanced at Maria but stood up and followed Rebecca when she failed to answer. "Everything's all right, isn't it?"

"Yes, of course." Rebecca's smile returned. "I suppose I expected things to stay the same forever, but once you're married, well, the magic goes."

"I keep telling Nell that, but will she listen?"

"In what way?" Nell's forehead creased. "Have you fallen out of love?"

Rebecca paused. "No, not at all. I still love the man I met."

"Ah, well, that's all right then." Nell's smile reappeared and she scurried into the living room to collect the plates. "Let me help you here and then we'd better be going."

"There's no need." Rebecca checked the clock. "I've plenty of time before Hugh gets home and it gives me something to do."

"If you're sure you don't mind. We'll see you next week."

Billy and Vernon were playing with a ball outside the house when Nell and Maria arrived home, but as soon as they turned the corner, Vernon ran to them, circled around and ran back to Billy.

"Where've you been?"

"Visiting Aunty Rebecca in her new house. You could have let yourselves in."

"We did, that was how we knew you were out." Billy

stood by the door waiting for them to go in. "May we have some biscuits?"

Maria raised an eyebrow at them. "You mean you haven't helped yourselves already."

Two innocent faces stared up at her as Billy spoke. "No, promise we haven't."

Maria nodded. "All right, one each, but don't go disappearing. Tea won't be long."

Nell set about putting the cloth on the table while Maria busied herself in the scullery.

"Did you ever ask George about moving? You said you didn't want to be in this house by next winter."

Maria snorted. "No, I couldn't bring myself to mention it. Besides, we won't need to move any more."

"Why not?" Nell collected the butter and jam Maria had lifted out.

"Because the main reason for moving was because the boys are growing and we were short of space, but Rebecca's gone now and I expect you'll be leaving once you're married. We'll end up with more room than we need."

Nell wandered back to the table. "I hadn't thought of that, not that I've any idea where we'll live."

"Didn't Jack mention anything?"

"No." Nell returned to the scullery and picked up a wooden board with a new loaf sitting on it. "He did say something to James..." Her heart sank as the words were out. *What on earth did I say that for?* She scurried back to the living room, but Maria followed her.

"Why would he tell James and not you?"

"I-I don't know. He didn't tell him where we'd live, it was probably idle chat in the alehouse."

Maria wiped her hands on her apron. "Yes, most likely. They do most of their business in there. So, you don't know what he said?"

Nell shook her head. "I didn't think to ask." She jumped as the front door opened and James walked in.

"Evening Aunty Nell, Mam." He took his usual seat by the fire. "Have you had a nice day?"

Nell smiled. "We called on Aunty Rebecca in her new house. It's lovely."

"I bet it is." He stretched out his legs. "I must call myself when I get chance."

"We were saying that Aunty Nell will probably leave us once she's married. She doesn't know if Jack has any plans for where they'll live, but thought he might have said something to you." Maria studied her son.

"Me?" James' eyes widened as he looked at Nell. "Why would he tell me?"

Nell grimaced behind Maria's back. "You're right, it makes no sense. I must be mistaken."

"Perhaps it was Tom he told?" Maria wandered to the table to pour James a cup of tea. "Those two were as thick as thieves when he was last here."

"Yes, that must be it." James winked at Nell. "I'll ask him next time I see him."

"That would be nice, although as long as we don't have to live in his room on Windsor Street, I'll be happy. Rebecca had to do that with Mr Grayson when they were first married and she hated it."

James shook his head. "I don't think he'll do that."

"He'd better not." Maria handed him his tea. "I expect

him to have a job and a house by the time you get married. Start as you mean to go on, that's what I say."

"Stop worrying. I'm sure he'll have something in mind and just hasn't told me." She bit her lip as her eyes flicked to Maria. *At least I hope he has.*

CHAPTER 15

J ack stepped onto the quay and removed his cap before running an arm across his forehead. He hated this hot weather almost as much as he did the cold, but he shouldn't grumble. It was nice to feel solid ground under his feet, and he was determined to make the most of it.

With the sun high in the sky, he glanced at the letter in his hand. The quick turnaround times at the ports they'd visited meant he'd not written to Nell as much as he'd hoped, and he needed to get this onto the next mail ship back to England.

He walked along the quayside, studying the ships that were being offloaded, painting a picture of them in his mind as he went. The river was narrow compared to the Mersey he was used to and appeared even narrower by having ships docked on both banks. Most of them were swarming with men moving barrels and crates from ship to shore, or back again. He stood and watched with a smile as the Chinese junks slipped in and out of the magnificent ocean-going sailing ships. He hoped that by giving Nell a sense of where he was, it would make up for the main news in the letter. His stomach churned as he thought about it and he glanced at the letter again, wondering, not for the first time, if he should post it. *Yes, you should. Nell has a right to know what's happening, even if it does upset her.*

He sighed and took the steps up to the main street where he paused to get his bearings. He rarely needed to send a letter home, but the captain had said the mail office was on the right-hand side if he walked along the Bund with the river on his left. The instructions were clear enough, but the bustle of the streets and the undecipherable writing on the shopfronts made it impossible to pick out what he was looking for.

Keep going to the left and you'll come to it.

He ambled along the footpath, blocking the way of many of the locals as he stopped and peered into each shop, but eventually the building he wanted came into view. It sat like an English outpost on the corner of the street, exactly as the captain had described.

The door had been propped open, and he peered inside to see an Englishman behind a battered old counter with a queue of sailors waiting to be served. He stepped through the door and took his place behind them, marvelling at how such a place could make him think of home. He couldn't put a finger on what it was, maybe the pictures on the wall. Or perhaps the grandfather clock that had pride of place in one corner. Either way, he suddenly longed to be home again.

The queue moved slowly, but as he approached the counter, he raised his face to a fan on the ceiling that wafted backwards and forwards as a young Chinese boy pulled on the rope attached to it. He let out a low groan. *That's nice.*

He took out a handkerchief and wiped his face and neck, reluctant to move forward away from the breeze. As the men in front of him disappeared, he had no choice and the man behind the counter looked up from his ledger.

"Good afternoon, sir. How may I help?"

Jack placed the letter on the desk. "Can this go on the first ship back to England; Liverpool if possible?"

The man smiled. "We've a steamship leaving tomorrow and travelling through the Suez Canal. It should arrive in Liverpool in about seven weeks." He checked a piece of paper on the counter. "That will make it the end of August."

Jack shook his head. "Amazing, I wish we could use the canal; life would be so much easier."

"You're on a sailing ship, are you?"

"I am, the *Flechero*, although I often wonder for how much longer. The way things are changing, the steamships will run us out of business."

The man stamped the letter and thrust it into a nearby bag. "I can't argue with that, sir. I'd make the most of it while you can."

"Yes, I will. I ... erm ... I don't suppose you have any letters for us, do you? I could take them back with me..."

The man checked a draw behind him. "No, there's nothing here. I seem to remember the captain calling yesterday and taking all we had. I'd check with him if you're expecting a letter."

Jack's shoulders sagged. "I'm sure he'd have passed it on, if there'd been one. Thank you, anyway." He bade the clerk farewell and squeezed past the queue that now extended out of the building. Stepping out into the searing heat, he held a hand above his eyes. *Seven weeks. What wouldn't I give to be home so quickly.*

He turned right out of the office and continued walking along the river. The captain had given him an hour on shore, and he was going to use every minute. They weren't due to sail for another three days, but they had a full cargo to load and he doubted he'd be able to leave the ship again. After that, they had stops all round the East China Sea before returning to Shanghai and travelling once again to Hong Kong to pick up their last cargo. Then they could head for home.

His heart was heavy as he thought of the journey home. It would take at least ten weeks once they left Hong Kong, assuming the winds were favourable, and that couldn't be guaranteed as the summer months approached the southern hemisphere. Even being optimistic, he knew it would be November before he was back in Liverpool. *I can only hope she waits for me.*

CHAPTER 16

James smiled as he released Nell's arm and stepped forward to knock on Rebecca's front door. He gave it three short, sharp raps.

"Should we go straight in?"

Nell grimaced. "I don't know. I would if I knew Rebecca was on her own, but I'm not sure we should if Mr Grayson's home."

"You're right. I wonder where they are, though." The smile dropped from his face as the door remained closed.

"I suppose they could have gone for a walk, although why they'd go out on such a warm day is beyond me. It was bad enough walking round here, and that didn't take long."

"Let me knock again. They may not have heard me." He'd banged on the knocker three times before Mr Grayson finally opened the door.

"Can I help you?"

"Good afternoon, Mr Grayson." Nell put on her best smile. "I hope you don't mind us visiting. May we come in?"

Mr Grayson flashed them a smile, but stayed where he was. "Rebecca's rather busy at the moment."

"Oh, that's a shame." Nell tried to peer into the house, but he'd pulled the door tight against his back.

"Who is it?" Rebecca's voice was cheerful behind him.

Mr Grayson stepped back into the room. "It's your sister and nephew."

"Let them in, then." A moment later, Rebecca pulled open the door. "Come on in. You don't need to wait."

"We weren't sure. We didn't want to disturb Mr Grayson..."

Rebecca held her husband's arm and gazed up at him. "Take no notice of him. He's being grumpy. Come and find a seat and I'll put the kettle on."

Nell hesitated as Mr Grayson's eyes fixed her to the spot. "Only if you're not too busy..."

"I'm not doing anything that can't wait. Just some mending."

"It needs to be done before I'm back at work." Mr Grayson curled his lip at Rebecca but she only tutted.

"And it will be. It won't take long, and I've all day tomorrow."

"Not all day, my dear. We'll be at church in the morning and evening, and we need dinner and tea in between times."

Nell picked up the handbag she'd placed on a chair. "I'm sorry, I don't want to cause any trouble. We'll come back one day in the week."

"Nonsense, we won't hear of it, will we?" Rebecca glared at her husband until Mr Grayson's shoulders dropped.

"No, of course not. Forgive me, but I worry about

Rebecca overdoing things. She has a rather weak constitution and I don't want her exhausted.

Since when? Nell watched Rebecca as she fluffed up the cushions on the chairs.

"Doing a spot of mending isn't going to drain my energy. Now, come and sit down while I put the kettle on."

James hadn't taken two steps from the front door, but as Mr Grayson sat down, he took the seat beside him.

"Good afternoon, Mr Grayson."

Mr Grayson inclined his head. "Good afternoon, Mr Atkin. It's very good of you to chaperone your aunt."

James grinned. "I don't mind. It gets me out of the house, and I was curious to see the houses around here. It's very nice."

"Yes, we're happy here..."

Nell hesitated as the two men settled in their seats, but followed Rebecca into the scullery. "Is everything all right?"

"Yes, it's fine; why wouldn't it be?"

Nell shrugged. "He didn't seem very pleased to see us."

"Oh, take no notice of him. He's not used to me wanting to spend so much time with the family." Rebecca disappeared into the living room to put the kettle on the range before coming back to retrieve a cake tin from the pantry.

"You'd tell me if there was a problem?"

"Of course I would, but there's nothing to tell."

Nell studied her sister as she focussed on arranging the cakes on a plate. "Is he the reason you don't call on us any more?"

"Now you're being silly."

"Then why haven't you called this week? Maria's worried about you."

"Oh, no reason. I've been busy."

Nell watched Rebecca flit around the scullery. "You said the house was easy to manage..."

"Nell, stop this." Rebecca glanced into the living room. "Everything's fine, so let it drop. I'll call round next week."

Nell took a step backwards as Rebecca thrust four plates into her hand.

"Take these through and I'll make the tea."

Nell's eyes didn't leave Mr Grayson as she joined them by the fire.

"Where've you been working?" James asked as Nell offered him a plate.

"In one of those big new houses on Princes Park. Several doors needed easing."

"Steady work for a carpenter, I imagine." James seemed relaxed, but Mr Grayson bristled.

"You'd think so, but the owner wasn't best pleased and took it out on us. We didn't even fit them..."

"Ah." James smiled as Nell returned with a plate of cakes and offered it to Mr Grayson.

"Do you see much of each other in the alehouse on Windsor Street?"

"No." Mr Grayson helped himself to a slice of fruit cake. "I stopped frequenting the place when we got married; there's an alehouse around the corner from here if I ever want to go out."

"And he likes it a lot." Rebecca smiled as she joined them.

"A man has to unwind after a hard day's work." Mr

Grayson spoke through gritted teeth, but Rebecca rolled her eyes.

"Don't get defensive, I'm not complaining."

Nell forced a smile as Rebecca disappeared back to the scullery. "It's a shame you're not closer to the one on Windsor Street. I'm sure James and my brother Tom would keep you company if you wanted the walk."

"I'm perfectly happy to stay closer to home; I can be back here within two minutes."

As you like. Nell took a deep breath. "Rebecca says you've no family around here. Are they all in Scotland?"

"I don't have family anywhere."

"Oh, I'm sorry. I'd no idea."

"You had no reason to. What's past is past, and the less said the better."

"Yes, quite." James raised an eyebrow at Nell. "So, which part of Scotland are you from?"

"Glasgow."

Rebecca returned with the teapot. "Don't you love his accent? It's one of the reasons I was attracted to him. I could sit and listen to him for hours."

Nell moved to the table to help Rebecca. "Yes, it's very pleasant."

"What brought you to Liverpool?" James asked.

"Work."

"Yes, of course. We're fortunate to have so much of it. Did you do your apprenticeship here?"

"No, in Glasgow. I moved down here when they wanted to put me on the ships."

"You moved to get away from the ships?"

"Aye."

Why would you come to Liverpool if you don't want to work on ships? Nell bit her tongue but James continued.

"I know what you mean. I'm currently apprenticed to be a carpenter, with the full expectation that I'll be a ship's carpenter like me dad."

Mr Grayson suddenly appeared interested. "And don't you want to go?"

"No, I hate the idea, but there's not much I can do about it at the moment. I'll have to finish me time."

"That's what I did, but as soon as I'd finished, they tried to press-gang me onto the ships. That was when I turned and ran."

"Why did you come to Liverpool then?"

Mr Grayson smiled. "I didn't want to move away from the sea, it's what I'm used to. I just didn't want to be *on* it. I came here with no past and set myself up as a carpenter."

"Isn't it strange how some men love going to sea, while others hate it?" Rebecca's gentle voice filled the room as she finally sat down and helped herself to a cake. "Nell's Jack loves it, doesn't he?"

Nell couldn't help smiling at the sound of his name. "He did, but he's giving it up when he gets home from this trip."

"Rebecca said he's in China."

"He was, but he should be well on his way home by now. I'm expecting him sometime in September."

Mr Grayson's eyebrows drew together. "It was March when he left, wasn't it? I wouldn't expect them to turn around and come straight back. Has he written to you?"

"I had a letter from him as soon as he reached Cape Town."

"But you've had nothing since?"

"Well, no. But they weren't stopping until they reached the Far East; I'm sure a letter's on its way." Nell sipped at her tea.

"I'd wait to see where the next letter comes from before you decide when he'll be back." Mr Grayson gazed over the top of Rebecca's head into the scullery. "I doubt he'll be home next month if you've not heard anything from China."

Rebecca's brow furrowed. "You seem to know a lot about it for someone who hasn't been to sea."

Mr Grayson's eyes pierced Rebecca. "My father was a sailor ... until the day he didn't come back."

Nell and James exchanged glances as the colour drained from Rebecca's face.

"Why've you never told me?"

"I try not to think about it." Mr Grayson stared straight ahead as Rebecca sat forward in her chair.

"I've asked you about your family, too. Why wouldn't you tell me?"

"I told you, I want to forget about it."

"Yes, of course. I'm sorry." She stood up again. "Let me top up the tea."

"Actually, we won't." Nell bit her lip as she placed her cup and saucer on the table. "We told Maria we wouldn't be long. Will we see you next week?"

Rebecca said nothing as she escorted them to the door and stepped outside with them. "I'll call around to yours, if I can. I'd like to see Maria. And Alice before she starts school."

CHAPTER 17

J ack lay on his bunk staring up at the ceiling. It had been a long day and although his body ached, his mind wouldn't sleep. Not after the news they'd received this afternoon. The ship rolled as a wave broke over it and Jack clung to the rail of the bed as water flooded down the steps. He'd better go and help. If this storm was still a couple of days away, it was going to be worse than they'd feared.

He grabbed his oilskins, fastening his coat tightly before he pulled himself up the stairs and braced himself as the rain pounded the deck. The light had long since disappeared and he clung to a guide rope as he made his way to the bridge where the captain was wrestling with the wheel.

"Do you think they got the timings wrong?" Jack shouted over the roar of the waves.

"I hope so. This rain can't get much heavier."

Jack clung to the railings as waves towered over the ship before crashing onto the deck. "Have you sent the men down below?"

"As many as I can spare. There's a couple tying up the last of the sails. We need to sit this out until it passes."

Jack peered towards the horizon, but the shoreline had disappeared. "We can't sit and wait. If the reports are right and the typhoon's still two days away, the ship won't last."

"I won't risk putting up the sails. They'll get torn to shreds."

"But we'll lose the whole ship if we don't move." Jack's throat croaked from shouting.

"Thank you, Second Mate Riley. I know what I'm doing."

"The wind will only get worse. We need to turn round and get out of its path."

"I spoke to Robertson earlier. We can't hope to make port without the risk of hitting the rocks. No. The three of us will take shifts to keep her steady until the worst of it passes."

The first mate knows no more about it than you do. "But that's madness." Jack's voice was lost as a wave crashed onto the deck. Seconds later there was a loud crack. "What was that?"

The captain pulled Jack back. "Take the helm and keep it as steady as you can. I'll go and take a look."

Jack fought with the wheel, clinging onto it as the wind swirled around them. With no gloves, his fingers were numb, and he wrapped his arms around the handles to stop them slipping from his grasp. He peered over his shoulder, but the rain blew straight into his face, obscuring even the poop deck. He rolled his shoulders and pulled his sou'wester further over his face as the water found its way down his collar. *Where is the captain?*

Eventually, after what felt like hours, he heard footsteps behind him.

"What's the matter?"

"We've damage to the hull..."

Jack leaned towards the captain as he struggled to hear.

"...leaking water."

"Are we likely to roll?"

"I've a couple of boys bailing... We've lost the mizzenmast ... wind caught the sail..."

Jack momentarily lost control of the wheel and scrambled to stop it spinning. "We can't stay here; we need to head further north and find shelter."

The captain finally nodded. "Turn her round; I'll check the charts." He turned to leave but stopped and shouted back to Jack. "And start praying."

Four hours later, Jack handed the wheel to First Mate Robertson and slumped onto a step behind him.

"At least the wind's weakening."

Robertson's sodden figure shuddered in front of him. "Not by much. I thought I'd lost her when that wave broke over the stern."

"We would have done if it had hit the side. It would have rolled us." Jack put his head in his hands as the boat lurched once more. "Let's hope we're over the worst of it. We can't head south until it's passed."

"We won't be going far, whatever the weather, with a broken mast and water pouring in. We'll have to stop at the nearest port and get the damage mended."

Jack's head fell forward as reality dawned on him, and he ran his hands over his eyes. *This will delay us by at least a month ... and I didn't tell Nell the truth in the first place.* He pushed himself up and lumbered back to his bunk. *This could be the end before we even start.*

CHAPTER 18

The postman was always as regular as clockwork. At eight o'clock each morning, he'd walk along Newton Street with a stack of letters and stop outside number three. Nell was always in the window waiting for him, her heart pounding with excitement, until the moment he shook his head and walked to the house next door. After that, her shoulders would droop and she'd wander aimlessly to the breakfast table, consoling herself only with a slice of bread and butter, and some sweet tea.

After nearly three weeks, it was a ritual she was tiring of, but she couldn't give up. Jack had promised. With five minutes to spare, she hurried down the stairs and took her seat by the window while Maria stood at the front door watching the boys head off to school. Once she was satisfied they were on their way, she closed the door and returned to Alice at the table.

"Are you still holding out hope of a letter?" Maria wiped Alice's fingers and sent her for her coat. "It's been months since he wrote. Why don't you accept that he's not the writing type and have something to eat? If the postman brings anything, you'll see it soon enough."

"He will write, and I like to wait so I know the postman's been. At least if I see him, I can relax and not be on tenterhooks for another four hours."

Maria shook her head. "As the saying goes, a watched pot never boils. If he's written, the letter will arrive when it arrives."

Nell sighed. "I suppose you're right." She stood up and gave one last look out of the window. "He's here ... and he's got something for us." She flung open the front door, her eyes wide as he handed her a manila envelope. "This is it. Thank you!"

As soon as she shut the door, she studied the letter. "It's from Jack. I recognise his handwriting." She grinned down at the letter. "I told you he'd write. What's the date on it? July the eighth. It's taken nearly two months to get here."

She returned to the seat by the window and sliced open the top as carefully as she could.

My dearest Nell

How I hope that you are safe and well and still think of me during our time apart.

Tears welled in her eyes as she read. Of course she remembered. She wiped her eyes with the back of her hand.

I'm missing you so much and am counting the days until I can hold you in my arms again. I've never realised how lonely it can be on a ship.

Nell let out a sob but coughed quickly, hoping Maria hadn't noticed.

We docked in... She struggled over the next word. *Sh-ang-hai?* She shrugged and continued to run her finger under each word. *China, yesterday.* Her smile returned. *It's so hot here, but I'm taking in as many of the sights as I'm able and hope to thrill you with my tales when we are next together.*

I don't yet have a date for my return. When we leave here, we travel north to Korea and Japan, then come back to Shanghai. We'll head for home after that, stopping only in Hong Kong to pick up our final consignment.

"He has to go to Japan!" Nell whimpered as she glanced over to Maria. "He hadn't left China when he wrote this and still needed to go north to somewhere I've never heard of, and Japan. That's even further away, isn't it?"

"I've no idea." Maria's brow furrowed. "I don't remember George mentioning it."

"I'm sure Jack said it was, when he was telling me about the places he'd visited." Big fat tears fell onto Nell's cheeks. "He's never going to get home, is he?"

Maria put a hand on her shoulder. "I told you, it's hard being a sailor's widow, even if you're not yet married. That's why I want you to be sure."

"I am sure. I just want him home so he can get a new job and we can put this behind us." She buried her face in her hands. "I wish George was here to tell me how long it takes to get back from Japan."

Maria coaxed her into standing up. "Come and have a cup of tea. We can ask James tonight when he gets home. It's as well Jack didn't give you a date; it would raise your hopes too much. Besides, if he posted the letter two months ago, I imagine he's well on his way by now. My guess is that he'll be here for Christmas; why don't we focus on that?"

"But Christmas is months off; it's not even October yet."

"Which means there's every chance he'll be back by then. If you expect him sooner, you're likely to be disappointed." Maria stirred an extra spoonful of sugar into Nell's tea and pushed it towards her. "At least you know he's safe and thinking of you."

Nell clutched the cup as it rested on its saucer. "Or he was in July."

"Stop fretting and get that bread eaten. You'll be no good to him when he gets back if you've wasted away." Maria passed her a jar of jam. "Here, put some of this on, it will help it go down."

Nell dipped her knife into the homemade plum jam and scraped a layer over the butter. "He's never mentioned going to Japan before."

"Sometimes they don't tell us these things, because they don't want to worry us. What they fail to realise is that if we don't know, we worry all the more."

Nell nodded. "You're right. When will they learn?"

Maria laughed. "You're still too young if you're saying things like that. When you get to my age, you'll realise they never do. Come on, eat up while I take Alice to school."

As soon as Maria disappeared, Nell took out the letter and straightened it out on the table. She hadn't read to the end. *Now, where was I?*

I understand if you're upset, but believe me, not as much as I am. I long to get home and make you my wife. I only pray that you'll wait for me.

All my love.

Your dearest Jack

Nell's forehead creased. *Why does he think I'll forget about him?* He'd mentioned it twice. She reread the letter

125

but the smile only returned to her face as she studied the envelope. Maria was right. He'd posted it in July, and so he was probably halfway home by now. *He should be back well before Christmas, and at least he still wants to marry me. I'd better hurry Rebecca with my dress in case he's early. What will he think if he arrives home and I'm not ready?*

A thrill coursed through her body as she read the letter twice more. Very soon now, she would be Mrs Jack Riley, and nobody, not even Maria, was going to stop her.

CHAPTER 19

The sun sparkled on the surface of the sea as waves lapped gently around the edge of the ship. The mainsail attracted what little breeze there was to bring them into the port. It really was perfect. Jack stood on the deck and held a hand above his eyes to protect them from the glare. He wanted to remember this view and recall it on the long winter nights when he was at home with Nell.

The mountains rose to ominous heights as they sailed towards Hong Kong Island, but as the ship followed the curve of the land, his stomach churned. So, this was why they'd not been able to sail for the last week. Reports had mentioned that Hong Kong had been in the direct line of the storm, but it had meant little. Until now. Jack stared at the devastation of what had been a thriving port last time they were here, only months earlier. Men were working now to clear the debris, as buildings stood without roofs, and many of the moorings and piers he remembered from previous visits were missing.

First Mate Robertson joined him on the deck. "It's as

well we weren't a day earlier when we made our initial approach. We'd have been in the middle of this."

Despite the heat, Jack shuddered. "God was watching us that day for sure, even though it didn't feel like it at the time."

"At least we're here now. We'll drop anchor a little further up on the left." Robertson pointed to several small cargo junks that were making their way to an area ahead. "It won't be easy, loading and unloading with so few piers, so we'd better get on with it."

The sound of the chains clanging as the anchor dropped jolted Jack and the first mate from their thoughts.

"We'd better go." Jack headed towards the front of the ship. "Do you know if we're allowed off?"

"I imagine we will be, although the captain's not said anything. He needs to find the cargo we're supposed to be taking back to Liverpool." Mr Robertson surveyed the bay. "Judging by the mess, it wouldn't surprise me if we have to wait for it."

As the sun set over the harbour, the captain called Jack and Mr Robertson to his quarters and offered them both a seat as he poured three shots of rum.

"I've been told we're likely to be here for a couple of weeks."

"Weeks!" Jack choked on his drink.

"I'm afraid so. We can't go back to England without a full load of cotton, but the storm damaged the consignment we were due to carry. They need to send another load."

Jack stood up and paced the room. "We're not likely to be home this year then?"

"I didn't know you were in a hurry, Mr Riley. You're not married, are you?"

"No, sir."

"Not to worry then, let's make the most of our time here. We'll get this cargo unloaded over the next day or two and then you, Mr Riley, can continue your studies for your first-mate exams. No point wasting the time you've been given, especially when you have me and Mr Robertson to help you."

"Yes, sir. Thank you. I'm sure it will be useful. Will I be able to go ashore, too? I have a letter to post ... and hopefully collect."

"I imagine so, but clear it with me first."

Jack nodded and helped himself to another shot of rum. *This is all I need. At least he wants me to study. I may end up being a first mate after all.*

CHAPTER 20

Nell gave the Christmas pudding a final stir and pushed the mixing bowl across the table to Maria.

"There we are; that should do it, although I imagine you can guess what I wished for."

"I'd have thought you'd be praying rather than wishing."

Nell pursed her lips. "There's no harm in doing both. Now, Alice, are you ready?"

Alice nodded and showed Nell the silver sixpence she clutched in her hand.

"Drop it into the bowl then."

Alice giggled as the coin fell onto the top of the mixture and she poked it in with her finger.

"I'm so looking forward to eating this." A smile broke across Nell's face. "I can almost taste it, but it will be extra special being able to share it with Jack. It's going to be the best Christmas ever."

Maria shook her head as Alice sat back down. "Whether Jack's here or not, we'll need to get it cooked first. Will you fetch the other bowl?"

Nell hurried to the scullery and came back with an already greased basin. "Here we are. Let's get the mixture in and it can go straight into the pan. The water's almost at the boil."

Nell tapped her fingers on the back of a chair as Alice insisted on helping, and as soon as they tied the string, she carried it to the top of the range.

"That's a good job done." She rejoined Maria to help tidy the table. "Shall we make the mincemeat next?"

"Give me a minute." Maria sat down while Nell wiped the table. "I'm not as young as you."

Nell laughed. "But you've been doing Christmas for a lot longer, so you know what you're doing. I need to learn. This time next year, I'll be doing it myself."

Nell couldn't keep the smile off her face, but Maria scowled.

"I'd assumed you'd still come here for Christmas. You can't spend it just the two of you."

"I'll still need to make my own mince pies and cake, though." Nell's brow creased. "I'd better check what Jack wants to do. He's never mentioned where he usually spends Christmas."

"I imagine he's been away for the last few years."

Nell nodded as she straightened up from the table. "I don't know what he did before he went to sea. He has a sister, so I'd better check he doesn't want to spend it with her."

"You've a whole year to think of that. I'm more concerned with this year," Maria grumbled. "Rebecca still hasn't told me what she's doing. I've invited her and Mr Grayson here, obviously, but she suspects Mr Grayson wants to stay at home." Maria shook her head. "I wish I knew what we've done to upset him."

"Are you sure it's us? He's never been friendly. Even at the wedding, it was an effort for him to talk to us. I thought that once they were married, we'd see more of him, but he's not interested."

Maria snorted. "I'm not so much bothered about him, it's the way he wants to keep Rebecca to himself that worries me. We've hardly seen her."

"I know and I miss her." Nell's shoulders dropped as she headed back to the scullery.

"It's a shame George or Jack aren't here. They'd get more sense out of him than we can, especially if he calls into the alehouse."

"Except..." Nell popped her head back into the living room. "He told James he doesn't go to that alehouse any more. He goes to one closer to home. Should we ask James to go and find him?"

Maria shook her head. "I don't think he's up to the task. He's too young. I'm afraid we need George ... or possibly even Jack. He can talk the hind leg off a donkey."

"At least we've not long to wait." Nell couldn't stop the smile returning. "If Jack isn't home this week, I'm sure he will be the one after. I can't believe it's nearly here."

Maria rolled her eyes. "The letter from Hong Kong said it would be early December, that's not next week."

"No, but it's the week after, and if the winds are doing their job, he may be early."

"I've already told you not to build up your hopes. I've learned the hard way that the ships are more likely to be delayed than be running ahead of time."

Nell clasped her hands together. "I don't care. Either way, he'll be here soon. These last eight months have been horrible, but it's almost worth it for the excitement of seeing him again."

Maria shook her head as she took over making the tea. "Well, enjoy it while it lasts. The worst thing is, you look forward to them coming home, but they've never missed you as much as you miss them, and before you know it, they're on their way again."

"But Jack isn't going anywhere. That's why it's so special. I get this wonderful feeling of knowing he'll be here any day now, and that he won't be going away ever again."

Maria carried the teapot to the table. "I can't deny I envy you that, although I suppose the day will come when George decides he's had enough."

"You don't have to wait too long for him, though. He should be back in the spring."

"Listen to you saying the spring isn't far off. You were beside yourself in September when I said Jack wouldn't be here until Christmas. It's not much different."

"Perhaps, but the time's gone quickly..." Nell had no sooner taken a seat at the table when the front door opened and Rebecca popped her head around the door.

"May I come in?"

"Of course you may." Nell immediately jumped to her feet again. "What are you doing here?"

"That's a fine welcome. You said I could call whenever I wanted."

Nell laughed. "You can, but I wasn't expecting to see you on a Sunday. I thought Mr Grayson liked you to himself."

Rebecca sighed as she took a seat. "He does usually, but I persuaded him to walk me here. He's gone to the alehouse while he waits."

"Couldn't you have come by yourself?" Maria studied her sister as she reached into the dresser for an extra cup and saucer.

"No." Rebecca's eyes flicked between her sisters. "He doesn't think it's safe for me to be out on my own. He's very sweet like that."

Nell took the seat beside her. "Is that why we never see you round here?"

"How can it be?" Maria handed Rebecca a cup of tea. "Mr Grayson doesn't know where she is while he's at work."

"No ... how could he?" Rebecca's voice was weak as she stared at her tea.

"Rebecca, look at me." Nell reached for her sister's hand. "Are you telling us everything?"

"Yes, of course." Rebecca pulled her hand away and stood up. "I have things to do. Anyway, I didn't call for a chat. I've come to tell you I've stitched your dress together, and it's ready to try on. We need to have a proper fitting."

Nell clapped her hands together. "Oh, how exciting! We'll need to get it finished quickly. Jack should be home in the next week or two, so I'm still hoping the wedding will be before Christmas."

"Oh gracious, I wish you'd warned me, I'd better get a move on."

"Shall we go to your house now, then? While Mr Grayson's out?" Nell stood up to go for her hat and cloak.

"There's no need for that." Rebecca chuckled as Nell's

cheeks coloured. "I'm sorry, I shouldn't laugh, but we needn't go straight away; I'd rather not rush the fitting."

"No, me neither, but once Jack's home, the dress will need to be ready."

"And it will be. It's looking lovely. You're going to make him glad he's not going back to sea."

Nell pouted. "I wish I was as clever as you at needlework. I don't think I'm good at anything."

"Nonsense. You're good at plenty of things..." Rebecca hadn't finished her sentence when there was a knock on the door and Maria stood up to answer it.

"Who on earth's this knocking?"

Rebecca took a mouthful of tea. "It will be Hugh. He said he'd pick me up on the way home. He wants to walk to the park..."

Nell's forehead creased. "But you haven't been here long."

"Mr Grayson, do come in." Maria put on her best voice as she opened the door.

"I won't if you don't mind, Mrs Atkin. Is Rebecca ready?"

"Erm ... yes."

"Yes, I'm here." She grabbed for her cloak. "Just let me fasten this; I'll see you tomorrow, Nell."

Without another word, Rebecca disappeared to join Mr Grayson.

"He must have guzzled that ale down pretty quickly, if he even had one." Maria peered down the street after them before she closed the door. "Why couldn't he let her stay for longer?"

"Rebecca said he wanted to go for a walk."

"A likely story." Maria retook her seat at the table. "He didn't want her to stay here."

"It's nice he's so protective of her, though." Nell stacked the dirty plates.

Maria shook her head. "It's not nice; it's frightening."

"Frightening?"

Maria shuddered. "I think I was wrong when I said Mr Grayson doesn't know what she's doing while he's at work. Judging by her response, it wouldn't surprise me if he has someone watching her."

"No!" Nell's eyes were wide as Maria held her gaze.

"I fear the carefree sister we used to know has gone. And there's not a thing we can do about it."

CHAPTER 21

The air was chill as Nell stepped outside to scrub the front doorstep. The ice had returned, and she imagined it would be a shock for Jack after the warm temperatures of China. Not that he'd mind if he could sit by the fire while she fetched and carried for him. Her heart pounded at the thought of it. *He'll be here any day now. I hope it's the same as it was before he went away.*

Her fingers were numb by the time she'd finished, and she stood up to throw the water from the bucket into the gutter.

"Are you only just finishing?"

Nell turned to see Rebecca walking towards her. "I wasn't expecting you, on your own, too."

"No, well... What have you been doing to make you so late?"

Nell opened the front door and ushered Rebecca inside. "We gave the house a thorough clean this morning, ready for Christmas. What brings you here?"

"A few things." There was a twinkle in Rebecca's eyes. "Firstly, your dress. It's almost finished."

"Really?" Nell grinned.

"Really, but I want you to try it on to make sure there are no last-minute problems."

"I can do that." Nell walked to the table and felt the teapot. "We should be able to squeeze a couple of cups out of that, but I'll put the kettle on again, anyway."

"Where's Maria?"

"She's gone to pick Alice up from school. She shouldn't be long, now."

"Of course, I keep forgetting she's growing up."

"It's because we don't see enough of you." Nell indicated for Rebecca to sit by the fire. "Do you want me to come to your house to see the dress?"

"That's the question. You can, but I was hoping I could bring it here."

Nell handed her a cup of tea. "There's more room at your house. Why can't you keep it there?"

Rebecca put down her tea. "It's Hugh. He's told me I have to stop sewing, so I'd rather keep it out of his way."

Nell's forehead creased as she took the seat opposite. "But that's terrible."

"It's not so bad, I don't need to stop completely, but he doesn't want me making things for money. Or for anyone else, even if they're not paying. He says he should provide for me..."

"I'm sure we could all do with the extra money if we had the chance. Are you sure he's not trying to cut off what bit of independence you have?"

"I don't think so." A twinkle appeared in Rebecca's eyes. "I've been to see the doctor."

Nell's face dropped. "Are you ill?"

"No, silly." Rebecca giggled. "I'm going to be a mam."

Nell put a hand over her mouth to suppress a squeal. "But that's wonderful."

"I know. I've been feeling sickly for the last few weeks and so I arranged a visit for yesterday. He said the baby will be born sometime in May next year."

"You must be thrilled. I know I will be when it's my turn."

"I've not stopped smiling; well, not while I've been on my own, anyway."

Nell raised an eyebrow. "What do you mean? Isn't Mr Grayson pleased?"

Rebecca's smile dropped. "I can't tell. He doesn't show many emotions, but no, he doesn't seem very happy."

"Can't you ask him why?"

Rebecca shook her head. "He was more bothered about me stopping sewing because I shouldn't be doing too much. I suppose he's only trying to take care of me."

"I imagine he'll still want you to keep the house clean, though. You need more energy to do that than you do to sew."

"But I can't do both, apparently. He'd already told me the house wasn't as clean as it should be because I went out too much..."

"But you hardly ever go out." Nell raised an eyebrow.

Rebecca sighed. "I probably spent too long at the shop. I know he likes things tidy but now there's a baby on the way, he's treating me like an invalid..."

"Perhaps things will improve once he gets used to the idea?"

"I hope so."

"Come on, cheer up, Maria will be here soon and I'm sure she'll be delighted."

"You're right." Rebecca's smile returned and she rested her hands on her belly. "Can you believe it? I'll be a real woman at last."

"I'm so jealous, but hopefully I've not got long to wait." Nell retook her seat. "You'll make a lovely mam. Will he let you do any knitting? I'll make a start if he won't."

"He'll have to cut my hands off for that." Rebecca laughed but her smile quickly disappeared. "The thing is, I need to work out what to do with the dress. I don't want him to think I'm still working on it."

"Bring it around here, then. I'm sure we can find room, and it will cheer me up every time I see it." Nell sat back in her chair. "I wish I could book the church for the marriage service. I expected Jack to write when he passed through South Africa again so I'd know when he was arriving."

"Haven't you heard from him since China?"

"No, but James says that even if he'd posted a letter from Cape Town, it would only arrive a few days ahead of him. He said there are no shortcuts from there, so depending on their stopover, it may not have been worth sending one."

"So, he could be home by this time next week, you just don't know it."

"That's what I'm hoping. At the very least, he should be home for Christmas." Nell paused as the front door opened and Alice ran into the room.

"Aunty Becca."

Rebecca wrapped her arms around her as Maria closed the door.

"My hands are so cold they're not working properly." Maria clenched and unclenched her fists as she walked to the fire. "Good afternoon, stranger. What brings you here?"

"I have some news." Her eyes sparkled as she sat Alice on her knee. "I'm going to be a mam!"

A smile cracked Maria's face. "That's lovely. I was beginning to wonder what was keeping you."

Rebecca's cheeks flushed. "These things don't always happen straight away. It's only been six months."

"They do if you don't want them to, but that's beside the point." Maria helped herself to a cup of tea. "When's it due?"

"May."

"That's nice, a summer baby..."

Maria's words were cut short as the front door burst open and Billy and Vernon charged in.

"Keep that door shut." Without giving them a chance to go back, Maria strode across the room and slammed it behind them. "What's up with you two?"

"Nothing." Billy stood panting as Vernon sat himself on the floor. "We had a race ... and I won."

"I should think you did, you're a few years older than Vernon."

"I kept up with him though ... and we beat James."

"James is here?" Maria's forehead creased as she opened the front door and peered towards Windsor Street. "I don't see him."

"He was still on Parliament Street."

"And walking *very* slowly." Vernon sniggered at Billy. "He didn't even wave to us."

"He'd better have a good reason for sneaking off work." Maria closed the door again. "I hope he's not taking lessons off your Uncle Tom."

Nell's stomach churned as Maria disappeared into the scullery. *What's he up to?* She turned to study Billy. "Are you sure it was him? He wouldn't ignore you."

"Of course it was him. Wasn't it?" Billy nudged Vernon with his elbow as they took their seats at the table.

"We know what he looks like. He just didn't want us to see him."

"I bet he didn't." Maria bustled back into the living room. "Wait until I see Tom. He'll be getting James the sack."

"That's what he wants. Ow..." Vernon stared at his brother. "What did you do that for?"

"I didn't mean to." Billy mumbled into the glass of milk Maria handed him, but Vernon put his heel on the chair to rub his ankle.

"Well, it hurt."

"I'm sure it was an accident." Nell looked over to them. "How was school today?"

"Boring." Vernon clanked his glass onto the table. "We do the same thing *every* day."

"But that's how you learn." Rebecca stood up and reached for her cloak. "If you say something often enough, you remember it."

"I already remember."

"That's good, then. Right, I must be going." Rebecca

walked to the front door, which Maria had once again opened. "Will you call later in the week?"

"We will if we're wanted." Maria stepped out onto the footpath.

"You're always welcome in the week, you should know that by now." Rebecca rolled her eyes, but Maria wasn't paying attention as she peered down the road. "If the boys saw James on Parliament Street, he should be here by now. Where on earth is he?"

"I'm sure he won't be long." Rebecca waved as she left, but Nell put a finger to her lips and shook her head at the boys as Maria came back into the house.

"They must have been mistaken. Even if he was dawdling, he'd be home by now." Nell took a seat next to Vernon, but her stare failed to keep him quiet.

"We weren't..."

Billy elbowed his brother. "I suppose we could have been wrong."

"Could we?"

"Yes, the man was a long way behind us."

Maria studied the two of them. "That's a relief. You need to be more careful before you come home spreading stories like that. You might have got James into trouble."

The fire had burned down by the time the front door opened and roused Nell from her dozing. *What time is it?* She glanced at the clock. Five to eleven.

The light from the embers was enough for her to make out the shape of James as he closed the door behind him and crept towards the stairs. Nell sat up straight in her chair.

"Why don't you come and sit down?"

James flinched at the sound of her voice and stopped to peer in the direction of the glow. "What are you doing still up? I expected everyone to be in bed."

She waited for him to join her. "Thankfully for you, everyone else is, but I suppose that was the plan."

He studied his hands. "I didn't realise the time."

"When you've been in the alehouse for nearly seven hours? Wasn't that long enough?"

"Does Mam know?"

"Not at the moment. I persuaded Billy and Vernon to keep quiet and tell her they'd been mistaken when they thought they'd seen you. Is this your Uncle Tom's doing?"

"Not exactly, but he gave me the idea."

"What idea?"

He shook his head as he took a seat. "He suggested that if I got myself sacked from work, it would get me out of my apprenticeship."

Nell shook her head. "Wait until I see him, not to mention your mam if she finds out."

"You won't tell her, will you?" His eyes were wide.

"That's up to you. What will the shipping lines say if they find out you were sacked for shirking your duties? They'd hardly want you on a ship serving their first-class passengers, would they?"

"But they needn't know..."

"Don't be so silly. They'll need references from your current company."

"I didn't need any when I got the job earlier in the year."

"Because you didn't sign a contract. Do you think the shipping line wouldn't have checked up on you?"

James was silent as he stared at the floor.

"I thought the plan was to up and go one day, not ruin your reputation before you did."

"I've been thinking about it and decided this would be better. Dad couldn't complain about me taking a new job if the master kicked me out..."

"You think your dad would be happy to hear you'd been skiving off work to the point where you got the sack? He'd be furious. And frankly, I wouldn't blame him. What were you thinking?"

James shrugged. "I don't know. I'm fed up of being picked on at the yard."

"You're not the only person to be picked on, and you won't be the last, but you have to remember, you're still only seventeen. You know I support you being a steward, but you've plenty of time, so I suggest you stop this nonsense, put your head down and get a trade first. You're halfway through your training already. By the time you come of age, you'll be free from the indenture, and a qualified carpenter. You can then do what you like." James remained silent as Nell pushed herself from the chair. "Now think on. I'm going to bed."

CHAPTER 22

Nell took her now familiar seat by the window while she waited for the postman. Jack must've written to tell her he was coming home, so why hadn't the letter arrived? She turned to see Maria carrying the bread and butter for breakfast to the table.

"To think I was expecting him home today; I didn't imagine I'd still be waiting for a letter."

Maria bustled back to the scullery. "I don't know why you fixed your mind on today. I've told you, ships have more of a habit of being late rather than early, and you've had nothing from him to say when he's arriving."

"Because today made sense based on when he was leaving China."

"No sign of him, Aunty Nell?" James rounded the bottom of the stairs and took his seat at the table.

"No, not yet, although I suppose I'm a little early today."

James laughed. "You've been early all week. I hope Jack knows how much you've missed him."

Nell's shoulders dropped as she turned back to the window. "I'm not sure he does. I haven't been able to write to him with him being so far away. I never knew where he'd be."

"The shipping line would have sorted that out for you." James took a bite from his bread. "He probably thinks you've forgotten about him."

"Do you think so?" Nell's stomach sank. *Is that why he kept asking?* "I hope not."

"Don't say that, she's bad enough as it is." Maria bashed James on the arm as she took her seat. "What about calling at the shipping line on your way home tonight, to see if anything's been posted outside?"

"I suppose I could." He turned to smile at Nell. "Hopefully, I'll have some good news for you by teatime."

"You might not need to." Nell's voice squeaked as she jumped from her seat and opened the door to snatch an envelope from the postman's hand. "It's from Jack."

The postman took a step back.

"Oh, I'm sorry, forgive me for being so hasty. I've been waiting for this for months and got a little carried away."

He gave a brief salute. "I'll leave you to read it then. Good morning."

"Good morning." Nell slammed the door closed and returned to the chair, where she sliced open the envelope. "Here we are, this was posted ... at the end of October?" Her brow creased as she picked up the envelope and wandered over to James. "That's a Chinese mark, isn't it?"

"It is." James put his bread on a plate. "That suggests they didn't leave China until early November."

Nell's eyes raced across the letter for words she was familiar with. "No, not China; Hong Kong. Where's that?"

"At the bottom of China." James stared up at her. "I thought you said he was leaving at the end of September."

"That's what he told me." She sat down and tried to focus as tears welled up in her eyes.

"May I?" James reached for the letter and scanned it. "They were delayed because they had to wait for the cargo."

"Why wasn't it ready for them?" Nell's shoulders slumped.

"Let me see. He says the harbour was damaged by a storm, so I imagine that's what delayed everything."

"A storm?" Nell put a hand to her chest. "Do you think he's all right?"

"I would say so, given he posted this, but ... oh..." He handed Nell the last page.

"Mid-January?" Her mouth dropped open as tears ran down her cheeks. "H-he won't be home for Christmas."

"Is that what it says?" Maria stared at James, who nodded.

"If they didn't leave Hong Kong until the end of October, ten weeks would take us into January."

"Oh, Nell, I'm sorry." Maria put a hand on her sister's. "Really I am, but I tried to warn you."

"What's the matter?" Billy asked as he and Vernon charged downstairs and headed to the table.

"Nothing." Maria stood up. "You'd better get a move on. You'll be late for school at this rate."

"Can we take this with us?" Vernon waved a piece of bread and butter in the air.

"No!" Maria's mouth dropped. "What will the neighbours think?"

"They won't think anything, they'll be too busy getting their own children to school." James stood up and grabbed hold of his coat. "Let them take a piece and they can walk with me. You need to look after Aunty Nell." He strode to the door and held it open while Billy and Vernon ran through it. "I'll see you later."

Nell collapsed onto the table. "I was so excited..."

"I know you were, but the middle of January is only a month off."

"But I was expecting him today..." Nell shrugged Maria's hand from her shoulder. "And I wanted him home for Christmas."

Maria took the seat next to Nell and waited until she lifted her head.

"Why didn't he tell me they'd been in a storm?"

"I told you, they think we'll worry if they tell us everything. It doesn't occur to them that we worry if they say nothing."

"He may have been hurt."

"But he probably wasn't. Most ships pass through storms, and George has told me they're never as bad as the papers make out. At least he sent the letter afterwards, so he must be all right."

Nell nodded and sipped her tea.

"I'll tell you what, why don't we pay Rebecca a visit this afternoon? We've not seen her since we called last week."

"It doesn't help that Mr Grayson won't let her walk round."

Maria sighed. "On this occasion, I'll forgive him. She is

expecting their first child, so he's bound to be worried. Wait until she's on her third, though. He won't be so bothered then."

Nell wiped her eyes on her sleeve. "It is nice that he's so thoughtful. We should be grateful."

Maria opened her mouth to speak, but stopped and shook her head. "I still wish he'd let us visit more often."

The wind swirled around the street as Nell pulled the door closed behind them as they left for Rebecca's.

"Come along, we'd better get a move on if we don't want to be frozen by the time we get there."

Nell put her head into the wind. "I hope Mr Grayson isn't home. Knowing him, he'll keep us waiting on the doorstep."

"Rebecca said we can go straight in, so he'll have to throw us out again if he's not happy to see us."

Nell shivered. "He's a strange man."

"He's no idea how much they'll need us once this baby's born. I'll tell you one thing; he won't want to be washing nappies while Rebecca's nursing the baby."

The journey took a little under ten minutes and Nell knocked on the front door and immediately went in.

"Rebecca, are you there?" Nell walked to the fire and rubbed her hands together. "She must be out the back. We may as well make a pot of tea while we wait." She lifted the kettle from the range, but put it down again to feel the side. "It's already boiled."

Maria wandered to the bottom of the stairs. "Rebecca,

are you up there?" When there was no reply, she opened the back door. "I'll check out here. I won't be a minute."

Nell followed her into the scullery and reached for the cups and saucers before arranging them on a tray. *Where does she keep the sugar?* She searched the shelves, but stopped when she heard her name being called.

"Nell! Come quick."

She threw open the back door and ran to the privy where Maria was crouching over Rebecca.

"Give me a hand, she's fainted."

"Is she all right?" Nell stared as Rebecca lay on the floor, her face white.

"I don't know, but she's frozen. We need to get her inside."

Nell hesitated as she bent down to pick up her sister's feet. "I think she's cut herself, too; there's blood on her skirt."

"Leave that, we'll see to it later. Let's get her to the fire first."

Rebecca was a dead weight as they half lifted, half pulled her into the living room, and as soon as they were by the hearth, Nell dropped her feet onto the rug.

"Run upstairs and get a blanket, we need to warm her up." Maria held one of Rebecca's hands and rubbed it vigorously.

"Yes, right." Without hesitating, Nell raced up the stairs and dragged several blankets from the bed. She was on the bottom step when she threw one to Maria. "Here. Let's get her wrapped up."

They worked quickly, and within seconds, nothing could be seen of Rebecca other than her face.

"Is she breathing?" Nell's stomach churned as Maria lay beside her sister and wrapped an arm around her.

"She is, but we need to warm her up. She's frozen."

Nell stared at the pallid face and hesitated before she knelt beside her and rested her hands on her cheeks. "What was she doing out there if she felt faint?"

Maria said nothing as she knelt up to rub Rebecca's arms. "Come on, Rebecca, speak to me."

Nell watched in silence until Rebecca's eyelids fluttered and she began to stir.

"Rebecca. Can you hear me?"

"W-what hap...?"

"Ssshhh. Don't talk." Maria leaned over her. "You fainted."

Rebecca's eyes suddenly widened. "The pain ... the baby..." She tried to move, but Maria held her down.

"There, there. You stay where you are and warm up. Nell, the kettle's boiling. Take it to the scullery and make that pot of tea."

Nell gritted her teeth as she stood up. *Why do I have to go?*

"It's gone." Rebecca's voice was faint.

What's gone? Nell watched as Maria cradled Rebecca's head in her arms.

"You've plenty of time."

"Nooo. It can't be."

Nell's heart raced as she put the kettle on the draining board and leaned back against the door frame. *What's gone?* She turned round to check on Rebecca. *What do I do?* She closed her eyes to focus on her breathing, but flinched as Maria pushed past her and reached for the tap.

"What's keeping you? Thank goodness Rebecca had already boiled some water." Maria filled up a bowl with a mix of water from the tap and the kettle and hurried back to the living room to wipe Rebecca's face.

"Nell. The tea."

"Yes, of course." She grabbed the kettle, which was now half empty, and held it under the tap before carrying it back to the range. *Calm down.* Her hands shook as she went back for the tea caddy. *Deep breaths. She'll be fine.*

By the time Nell carried the teapot through to the table, Rebecca was leaning on a bank of pillows, her eyes closed.

"How is she?" Nell walked towards Maria. "Will she be all right?"

"She will, thankfully, but we'll have to stay with her until Mr Grayson gets home. We can't leave her."

"What happened? Do you know?"

Maria shook her head. "She won't say, but she's lost the baby."

"Lost it? Oh no." Nell dropped to the floor beside Rebecca, tears welling in her eyes. "She was so excited. She'd started knitting already." Nell reached behind her and pulled out a bag of wool. "Look, she'd already made some little bootees and a hat. It's so unfair."

"I'm afraid life's unfair." Maria stood up and poured milk into the cups as tears ran down Nell's cheeks. "These things happen."

"D-did it happen to you?" Nell turned away as a scowl crossed Maria's face. "I'm sorry, I shouldn't have asked."

Maria straightened the cups on the tray and poured the tea. "I suppose there's no harm telling you, you'll need to know these things soon enough. It did as it happens."

"Oh, I didn't know."

"You were too young." Maria picked up a cup and saucer. "As I said, these things happen, and it didn't stop me having a family ... although obviously we lost Fred. That was much worse."

Nell shook her head. "Young Fred. What a lovely boy he was."

"Exactly." Maria rubbed a hand across her eyes. "Unfortunately, it happens to many women; at least Rebecca's plenty of time for more."

Nell screwed up her eyes as Maria settled Rebecca into a chair by the fire. *Will that be my fate, too? I hope not.*

They hadn't finished their tea when the clock on the mantelpiece struck half past five and Mr Grayson arrived home. He closed the front door with a slam as his eyes flicked around the room.

"What's going on? I didn't know you were calling today."

Nell shrank back into her chair but Maria stood up to face him.

"No, but it's as well we did. I'm afraid Rebecca's in some distress; she's lost the baby."

His eyes rested on Rebecca as tears flowed down her cheeks.

"I'm sorry. I didn't do it on purpose."

Mr Grayson turned back to Maria as she twisted her fingers together.

"What did you do to her?"

"We didn't do anything?" Maria's voice was raised.

"When we arrived, she was on the ground in the backyard..."

"In this weather? She must have been frozen." His eyes bored into his wife. "What were you thinking?"

"I needed to use the privy ... there was a pain ... and then..."

"Why didn't you come back inside, you stupid woman? What have I told you about going outside?"

"Don't you dare talk to her like that." Maria stepped in front of Rebecca. "She fainted and collapsed to the ground. She didn't do it on purpose."

"She should never have been in the yard. I ordered her to stay in bed and not receive visitors..."

"You should be jolly glad we called. She might not be sitting there now if we hadn't."

"She wouldn't have been out of bed if you hadn't called..."

"Stop." Rebecca's voice was weak but sufficient to cause everyone to turn to face her. "I got the pains when I was in bed. I slipped on my dress so I could use the privy..."

"Why couldn't you use the chamber pot..."

"Mr Grayson, please..." Maria's voice was shrill. "I hardly think now's the time to argue about such matters. She's just lost your baby."

"And nearly died in the process because she went outside."

"You can't keep her indoors forever." Nell's hands shook as she knelt beside Rebecca. "But that's what you'd like to do, isn't it? Can't you see how miserable you're making her?"

"She's my wife and I won't take lectures from you."

"Mr Grayson, will you stop and listen to yourself?"

155

Maria stood with her hands on her hips. "Have you any idea what she's been through this afternoon?"

He paused for a moment before taking the seat opposite Rebecca. "I do as it happens." His voice dropped. "That's why I wanted to take care of her."

Nell's nostrils flared. "Well, you've a funny way of showing it."

"That's enough, Nell." Maria shot her a look. "It's very distressing at the moment, but I'm sure she'll be fine in a few weeks, and there's plenty of time for her to have another one..."

"No." Mr Grayson banged a hand on the chair. "There won't be any more. I've already told her, it's too dangerous."

Maria glanced at Nell and shrugged. "I'm sure it's perfectly normal."

"It's far too normal..." his head jerked up and held Maria's gaze "...and I won't lose my wife the same way as I lost my mother."

Nell's stomach somersaulted, but Rebecca's sudden movement distracted her.

"You can't stop me being a mam." She buried her face in her hands. "It's all I've ever wanted."

"And you're all I want." His tone softened as he knelt on the floor beside her. "I don't want to lose you." He stroked the top of her head, but she pulled away, her sobs filling the room.

"If I can't be a mam, I might as well be dead..."

"Now don't be silly." Maria offered her a handkerchief. "Wipe your face and take a deep breath. You'll get over this."

"I can't bear being on my own, day after day, seeing

nobody ... and there won't even be a child to look forward to." Rebecca rocked backwards and forwards, clutching her hands to her chest.

"We need to change that then, don't we, Mr Grayson?"

Mr Grayson pulled the blanket over Rebecca as Maria glared at him.

"You walk past the end of our road each morning on your way to work. Might I suggest you bring Rebecca to our house so she doesn't have to spend time on her own in this soulless place?" Maria inspected the spotless floor.

Mr Grayson pinched the bridge of his nose as he stood up. "Rebecca and I need to talk. If you don't mind; we'd like to be alone."

"Only if Rebecca doesn't mind." Nell squeezed her sister's hand, but stood up when she nodded.

"I'll be fine, as long as you promise to call tomorrow. I doubt I could walk to your house, the way I feel at the moment."

"Don't worry, we'll keep an eye on you from now on." Maria took her cloak from the wall and stared at Mr Grayson. "I invited you and Rebecca to our house for Christmas dinner, but she didn't give me an answer because she didn't want to upset you."

"I want to spend it together, just the two of us; not with a bunch of people who'd take her attention from me."

Maria stood with her hands on her hips. "I don't know what your problem is, but Rebecca's used to having family around her and after today, that's what she'll have. If you don't want to join us for Christmas, then so be it, but I expect to see Rebecca."

"You can't tell me what to do with my own wife."

Maria glared at him. "Do you want her to end up hating you? Because if you carry on treating her like this, that's exactly what will happen."

"You don't know that."

"Mr Grayson, Rebecca's my sister, and I've been like a mam to her for over fifteen years. I'll tell you now, it's happening already."

"No."

"All right, have it your way." Maria opened the door and beckoned for Nell to join her. "Let me tell you now though, if you expect me to abandon her to you, you can think again."

CHAPTER 23

The walk home from church was brisk, and Maria held open the door for Nell and closed it as soon as she and Alice were inside. Billy and Vernon were already in front of the fire drying out, but Vernon grumbled as Alice sat with them.

"It's supposed to snow on Christmas Day, not rain. We can't even play out in this."

"And a good thing, too. Today's a day for staying in and being together." Nell went to the back door and shook out her cloak.

"But that's boring."

"Less of your lip, young man." Maria shook her own cloak. "You've no time to play out. James will be back shortly with the goose and I want everything ready for when Aunty Rebecca arrives. You two can bring in the yule log and put some more coal on the fire."

"Do we have to?" Vernon huffed as he stood up. "My socks haven't dried out yet."

"Well, it's a good time to go if they're already damp."

Maria waited for them to go outside before she stepped into their places by the fire. "Let's see how the veg are doing." She stabbed at some carrots and parsnips with a knife. "They're done. I'll take them off the heat and you can warm the gin punch."

"I'll put the bread sauce to warm, too. Rebecca won't be long." Nell shuddered as the back door opened and Billy carried in the yule log.

"Shall I put it on?"

"No." Maria scurried to the table. "Leave it to one side and put more coal on the fire. James can place the log on when he gets back."

"Is the table all set?" Nell asked when Maria returned.

"Yes, we're all done; we're just waiting for the meat." Maria peered out of the back window. "I hope they wrap it up well. It wouldn't do to get it wet."

"I'm sure they will; I'm more bothered about Mr Grayson. How do you think he'll be today?"

Maria rolled her eyes. "Goodness knows. Rebecca said he'd been very good to her since the *incident*, and at least he agreed to join us today. I don't know whether he would have done otherwise."

"Let's hope the weather doesn't put him in a bad mood. That's all we need..."

The front door opened and a moment later James' voice filled the room. "Can someone come and take this from me?"

"One minute." Nell hurried to take the crate from him. "Oh good, it's still warm. Was the baker's busy?"

"It was; it's a good job he has a big oven." James turned to close the door but immediately opened it again. "Mr

Grayson, Aunty Rebecca. I'm sorry, I didn't see you out there. Merry Christmas."

"Merry Christmas." Mr Grayson ushered Rebecca into the room and extended his hand to James.

"And the same to you." Nell hugged her sister before Maria could muscle in. "I'm glad you could join us, Mr Grayson."

"Yes, well. Rebecca and I had a long talk..."

"About time." Maria took their coats. "Christmas is not the season to be sat at home on your own. Now, come and take a seat. I've made some gin punch."

"That sounds nice." Rebecca smiled as Mr Grayson held out a seat for her.

"It is." Maria chuckled and pointed to a large pan on the range. "I took the liberty of tasting it earlier. If I didn't have to make dinner, there might not be so much left."

"Well, let Hugh help you with it, then. It looks heavy."

Maria raised an eyebrow at Nell. "Only if you're sure. It's the one on the left-hand side."

Mr Grayson scowled at Rebecca but strode to the range and carried the pan to a thick wooden board on the table.

"Ah, thank you. Take a seat while I serve it out." Maria ladled a spoonful of warm gin punch into five glasses.

"There we are." She handed them around and raised her glass. "Merry Christmas and good health to all of us."

"And a speedy return for Jack." James clinked his glass onto Nell's. "It won't be long now."

Nell smiled. "No, only three weeks ... unless something else goes wrong."

Maria took her seat. "We don't want any talk like that today. It's a time for celebration."

"Absolutely." Mr Grayson stood up and banged his glass against everyone else's. "And for giving thanks."

Rebecca's brow furrowed as she stared up at him. "Thanks?"

"Of course, thanks. It's Christmas Day. The day of our Lord's birth. Whatever else has happened, we should be grateful."

Rebecca nodded but said nothing as Mr Grayson stayed on his feet.

"I'd also like to make a toast." He turned to Maria and Nell. "To Mrs Atkin and Miss Parry. Thank you. I realise now that without you, we might not be sitting here today."

"Why, what happened?" Vernon's whisper was rather loud and Billy nudged him.

"I don't know."

"You two behave yourselves." Maria raised her glass to Mr Grayson. "Here's to some good coming out of it then."

He clinked her glass again. "And here's to my undying gratitude. If it hadn't been for you, well..." He smiled again at Rebecca. "What I'm trying to say is, I apologise for the way I've behaved and you're welcome to visit us any time. Not having much of a family myself, I hadn't appreciated how much you help each other, but, well ... I know now that Rebecca needs more than me."

Nell smiled. "And we need her."

Maria nodded. "We won't be leaving her on her own, either. Not for the time being." Maria raised her glass again. "Here's to us all and a brighter future."

"To us all." James raised his glass but pulled a face as he took a mouthful of gin. "Urgh! I can't drink that; sorry,

Mam, but I'll have to switch to ale." He stood up to go to the pantry. "Would you prefer ale, Mr Grayson?"

Mr Grayson hesitated. "Well..."

"Have one if you like, we've plenty in the pantry." Maria winked at Nell. "Besides, if you don't like the punch, it means there's more for the rest of us."

Mr Grayson relaxed. "Very well then, thank you."

"When are we doing the presents?" Vernon asked. "You said we could have them after church, and that was ages ago."

"After dinner. We'll have this, then we'll eat, and then we'll open the presents. We've got all day, there's no rush."

Vernon's shoulders slumped. "I'm bored. Can't we play out? It's stopped raining."

"No, you cannot. Now, sit there and be patient."

Following the opening of the presents, James and Mr Grayson took the seats on either side of the fireplace as Maria and Nell tidied up.

"I must admit, I enjoyed myself more than I thought I would." Mr Grayson stretched out his legs as Rebecca handed him a glass of port.

"I'm glad." Maria wiped a cloth over the table. "Have you never had a family Christmas?"

"Not since I was a child. I lived with my nan until I was fourteen, and she always did her best, but once we lost her, I was on my own. Dad was still at sea and his sister, my aunty, had enough children of her own. They always invited me for dinner, but, well, I never felt welcome. Not like I have been here."

Nell felt a tinge of sympathy as Mr Grayson closed his eyes. *There's always someone worse off than you.*

"Are you sure you don't want to come to Tom and Sarah's?" Maria asked for the umpteenth time. "I'm sure they'd be delighted."

"I'm quite sure." Rebecca gave a weak smile. "It's been a lovely day, but I'm tired now."

Mr Grayson suddenly sat up. "You're right. The food and the fire were sending me into a slumber, but I need to get you home." He emptied his glass and handed it to Maria. "Thank you once again for a lovely day."

"You're welcome. Hopefully, you'll be able to make it to Tom's next year."

"Let's hope so." Rebecca gave her sister a hug. "I'll see you tomorrow."

Maria walked them to the door and watched them disappear before she rejoined the table. "That went better than expected."

"It did." Nell topped up their glasses. "Shall we finish this?"

Maria giggled. "It would be a shame to waste it. Vernon, what are you doing?"

Nell peered under the table to see Vernon recovering a stray marble.

"Nothing. These are great; we needed new ones."

Maria rolled her eyes as she sat beside Nell. "How are you doing?"

"I'm fine. Thank you for a nice day. I would never have thought Mr Grayson would relax like he did. It must have been the talking-to you gave him."

"I think the brandy in the white sauce helped. We must remember that if he stiffens up on us again."

"It's a good job I didn't have too much, then." Nell grinned as she gazed at the empty seat opposite James. "I could go to sleep myself."

"You haven't time; we need to be going out shortly."

"Can't we have half an hour?"

"No, we can't. Come along." Maria stood up and reached for Nell's hand, but James made no attempt to stand up.

"Have you been to see the vicar yet, Aunty Nell?"

"No, not yet. I'll go in the New Year. I can't do much until Jack's home. He's been delayed so many times, I don't even trust he'll be here in January. You will keep calling at the shipping line, won't you, in case there's any news?"

"I will." James smiled. "I'm looking forward to seeing him as much as you are."

Nell smiled. *I doubt that.* "I'm glad the two of you get along so well."

"I didn't think we would when I first met him; I thought he'd be a typical sailor, one who came ashore, caused havoc and left again, but he's not."

"No, he's not. But then neither's your dad, or half the men who live around here. It's only the foreigners, who've got nothing better to do than spend all their days and nights in the alehouses."

James nodded. "I wonder if Jack's like that when he's in other countries."

"I hope not!" Nell's face must have been a picture because James laughed at her.

"No, I didn't mean that, I meant, I wonder what he does

when he's ashore. I'm sure he won't be one of those who, you know ... does anything *improper*. In fact, I doubt they even have alehouses in places like China." He took a gulp of his ale as Nell's forehead creased.

"No, I don't suppose they do. I wonder what they have instead."

"That's enough of that." Maria took James' glass from him. "On your feet. There'll be a houseful waiting for us at Uncle Tom's, and hopefully, they'll do a better job of stopping Aunty Nell from worrying than you are."

CHAPTER 24

The final approach into Liverpool never ceased to amaze Jack. Less than two weeks ago, over Christmas, he'd been beyond hot as they sailed up the coast of Africa. The sun had been so high in the sky that they'd had no shade from the searing heat, and the crew had worked in nothing but their trousers. Now, sailing up the Irish Sea, he pulled his coat tightly around him and stuffed his hands in his pockets. Although it was early January, the sea was calm, which was a pleasant change from yesterday when they'd been off the coast of France in the Bay of Biscay. It had been its usual turbulent self, but after China, he hadn't heard any complaints.

He walked back to the helm where the captain was edging the wheel towards the right.

"Not long to go."

"No, sir. By this time tomorrow we should be back on shore."

"When's your next trip?" The captain didn't take his eyes from the sea.

"I don't have one planned, sir."

The captain turned to him. "None planned. Why not?"

Jack cleared his throat. "I ... erm ... I'm getting married, sir."

"Married? You kept that to yourself."

"Yes, sir. I've tried not to think about it; I didn't want any distractions." Jack hoped he sounded convincing, but the captain shook his head.

"These women always get in the way. I hope you're not giving up the sea for good."

"I'll get a land-based job when I'm home and see how it goes."

The captain gave a loud harrumph. "I doubt you'll be happy. You're a sailor; I told you that when we first met."

"Yes, sir." Jack stared out at the Welsh hills as they loomed ever larger. "I must admit, I'll miss days like this."

"At least you're all set to take your first-mate exams when you get to Liverpool. Don't let all that study go to waste. I expect you to pass with flying colours."

"No, sir, I won't. It may come in handy one day."

Nell wiped her hands on her apron as she stood up from the fireplace in the front bedroom. She certainly missed Rebecca's help with the cleaning, particularly on Mondays when the washing needed doing too. She picked up the bucket with its remains of soot and ash and sauntered downstairs to the scullery where Maria was stirring a large pan of stew.

"That scouse smells good." She opened the back door and hurried to the ash pit to empty the bucket.

"Are you finished?" Maria asked when she returned. "We may as well eat now."

"Let me get cleaned up and I'm all yours."

She hadn't reached the bottom of the stairs when there was a knock on the front door. "Who on earth's this?" With a quick wipe of her hands on her apron, she reached for the handle.

"Good morning, Nell."

"Jack!" Nell's eyes widened as she threw her arms around his neck as he clung tightly to her. "I can't believe you're here. Why didn't you tell me?"

His eyes twinkled in that instantly familiar way as he released his hold and reached for her hands. "I didn't want to disappoint you any further."

"Well, come in. Maria, guess who's here."

"Who is it?" Maria wandered into the living room. "Jack. Well, about time, too. Nell's only been waiting for you since September."

He squeezed Nell's hand. "I'm sorry, but after all the delays around China, I was nervous about giving you a date in case we were delayed again." He sniffed the air. "My, that smells good."

"He can join us for dinner ... can't he?" Nell's eyes pleaded with Maria.

"I imagine so, after all this time; come and take a seat." Maria watched Nell as she headed for the chair next to Jack. "I thought you were going to get cleaned up."

"Oh, yes." She glanced down at her dress. "Don't go

169

anywhere, I'll only be a minute." She raced up the stairs and hurried to the washstand in the bedroom. *Oh, gracious, look at the state of me. What must he think?*

She thrust her hands into the cold water and by the time she'd finished, it was black. *That will have to do, I've no time to get fresh water.* She retrieved a clean dress from the wardrobe and, following a swift flick of the brush over her dishevelled hair, she tied back the loose strands that had fallen across her face. *Finished.* Leaving her soiled dress in a heap on the floor, she raced to the top of the stairs, but stopped as she heard Maria talking.

"I won't give my blessing if you're likely to go away again. What about those fancy ideas you had about becoming a master mariner?"

"I've told you, I've changed my mind. What else can I say to convince you?"

"I want you to promise that you'll stay with her."

"I will."

Nell's heart pounded as the room fell silent, and after a moment's hesitation, she bounced down the stairs. "There, is that better?"

Jack smiled. "It doesn't matter to me what you wear, you always look lovely." He winked at her as Maria turned to go to the scullery. "What have you been up to while I've been away? I feared you'd forgotten about me when I didn't get any letters from you."

Nell's cheeks flushed. "Of course I didn't forget. Why would you think that?"

The smile stayed on his face, but his tone changed. "I got used to being the only one who didn't get any mail when we arrived in port."

"Seriously?" Nell's eyes were wide. "Oh, Jack, I'm sorry. It didn't occur to me to write; how would I know where you'd be?"

"The shipping company forward our mail. They generally know where we'll be in advance."

"I'd no idea..." She was about to take his hand when Maria walked in with two plates of scouse.

"Here, get that down you, and then Jack can tell us what plans he has, now he's back."

"Plans?" He held his knife and fork poised as he waited for Maria to bring in her own plate.

"Yes, plans. Have you got a job yet?"

"Give me a chance. I only arrived this morning and came straight here." He shovelled a forkful of scouse into his mouth.

"Let him eat before you bombard him with questions." Nell glowered at her sister. "This is probably the first proper meal he's had in months. Let him enjoy it."

"You're good to me." Jack smiled at her.

Maria picked up her knife and fork. "And don't you forget it."

With his plate empty, Jack wiped it clean with a piece of bread and sat back in his chair. "You're wrong about me."

Maria studied him. "You need to prove it. What sort of job's going to keep you happy for the next forty years?"

Jack shrugged. "I don't know yet. The captain was disappointed when I told him I wasn't going back to sea, but offered to have a word with the office to see if they have anything for me."

Nell beamed. "That's wonderful. Will you go in this afternoon?"

Jack laughed. "Give the captain time to speak to them. I said I'd call at the beginning of next week."

"What sort of thing might they have?" Maria's face refused to crack.

"I've no idea; I've never worked in an office. Something to do with ships, I should imagine."

"Don't you get lippy with me, Jack. If you don't know what jobs are available, how do you know you'll like them?"

"I don't, but I'll find out what's on offer and give it a try. What else can I do?"

Nell placed a hand on Jack's. "Does that mean we can visit the vicar?"

Maria glared at her. "You can't get married until he's found himself a suitable job."

"Why not?" Nell returned her sister's stare. "He'll get a job soon enough, so why can't we arrange the wedding at the same time? I've been waiting ten months for this."

"Where will you live, if he has no money?"

Jack stared at Maria over the rim of his teacup. "I am still here, and for your information, I've enough money to be getting on with. You know as well as I do that one of the benefits of being on a long voyage is that the wages are good. Besides, we can live in Windsor Street until we're ready to get our own house."

"Windsor Street? Are you sure?" Nell tried to hide her disappointment.

"Why not? That way we can be married as soon as the banns are read."

Her smile returned. "Really, so soon?"

"Whenever you like. I expect I'll have a job by this time next week, and I've already spoken to Mrs D about you moving in. All we need to do now is set the date."

CHAPTER 25

Nell stood at the top of the aisle and smoothed a hand down the front of her cream dress as Rebecca straightened out the train.

"You look wonderful." Tom smiled as he offered her his arm. "Jack's a lucky man."

Nell's cheeks coloured and she was glad to have the veil covering her face. "I'm the fortunate one." She gazed at Jack as he stood with his back to her, his top hat tucked beneath his arm. "There were times I didn't think this day would arrive."

"You needn't have worried; he was always going to come home." The church organ struck up the 'Bridal Chorus'. "Are you ready?"

"I've been ready for the last year." Nell squeezed her brother's hand. "Don't keep me waiting any longer."

Tom held his head high as he led Nell towards the altar, but she hesitated as they approached the front and Jack turned to smile at her. She kept her eyes fixed on his impish grin, but by the time he lifted her veil and gazed into her eyes, her heart was racing. *I love you, Jack.*

The service was short, with only two hymns and a bible reading, but she stumbled over the words as she recited her vows. *Why is it so difficult? Jack said his well enough.* She paused for breath. *I can do this.* Jack didn't take his eyes off her as the vicar repeated her line and she repeated it after him. *There, done.* She breathed a sigh of relief as the twinkle returned to Jack's eyes and they turned to watch the vicar bless the ring. Jack's touch was gentle as he slipped it onto her finger and repeated the vicar's words.

"With this ring I thee wed, with my body I thee worship, and with all my worldly goods I thee endow: In the Name of the Father, and of the Son, and of the Holy Ghost. Amen."

Nell smiled at the wedding band on her finger. That was it. It wouldn't be long now before they were alone in the privacy of their own room.

Once the formalities were over, Jack led her back down the aisle, but Nell stopped when they reached the doorway.

"What's the matter?" The concern in his eyes caused Nell to giggle.

"It's freezing out there, that's what's the matter. Have you noticed how thin this material is?" She shook her head. "I don't know what I was thinking wearing such a flimsy gown at the beginning of February."

Jack grinned. "I'll warm you up later."

"Jack!" She felt her cheeks colour and turned to make sure no one had heard him, but Jack only laughed.

"You're a married woman now."

"I might be, but we're still in church." She peered out through the door. "Shall we make a dash for the carriage?"

"You're not dashing anywhere in that dress." Rebecca appeared behind her. "Besides, we need to throw this." She waited for the rest of the congregation to gather before she counted to three, and confetti filled the air. Most of it landed on Nell, who brushed it from her shoulders.

"It will take me hours to get rid of this."

Rebecca laughed. "It took me days. Now, let me help you with your train."

Once they were seated in the carriage, Nell leaned back into Jack's arms. "Will I ever get used to feeling your arms around me?"

"I hope so." He squeezed her shoulders, but Nell turned, her eyes searching his.

"I understand now what Maria meant when she said how hard it would be if you were only home for a few weeks. After being without you for so long, I couldn't bear the thought of you leaving again so soon."

He tightened his grip on her as the carriage pulled away. "I don't know how many times I have to tell you, I'm not going anywhere."

Maria and Rebecca had put on a wonderful spread of food and Nell stood with Jack by the front door of the house waiting to greet their guests. James was the first to arrive with Billy and Vernon.

"Welcome to the family, Uncle Jack."

Jack laughed. "I think you can drop the uncle, I'm only ten years older than you."

"We'd better not while Mam's around, she's a stickler for using proper titles."

"All right, it's a deal. Just not in the alehouse."

Nell ran her eyes along the queue as it snaked out of the front door. "James, you'd better move along, we'll speak to you later."

Tom and Sarah were the next to arrive.

"I'm sorry we had to bring the whole family." Sarah held the youngest child on her hip, while two walked in without waiting, and two others clung to her skirt. "We're running out of people who'll have them all at once."

"I'm sure Maria won't mind. You know how she loves a houseful of children."

"That's a good idea. I'll see if she'll have a couple now."

Nell watched as Sarah handed over her youngest son. "It's a shame none of your family could come to the service. I've not met them yet."

Jack ran a hand over his head. "You will in good time; but it's too far to travel in this weather."

"West Derby's not that far, is it?"

"Far enough."

It took another five minutes for them to greet the rest of their guests, and as several neighbours brought up the rear of the queue, Nell was relieved to close the front door. She wandered to the fire where Jack had already made himself at home.

"I didn't see your landlady arrive, I thought you'd invited her."

"I did, and I saw her in church, but she must have gone back to the house. She has a room to prepare." Jack winked at her, but Nell's giggles stopped when Tom joined them.

"I believe you'll live on Windsor Street for the time being?"

"We will. I decided it was best to get a job before a house, so I know how much money I'll have to play with. At least I've got rid of my old room-mates." He grinned at Nell. "One only moved out this morning though, which is why I imagine Mrs Duffy will still be rearranging the room for us."

"You got the job with the shipping line, I believe."

"I did, I start first thing on Monday morning. When the captain heard I was giving up the sea, he put in a good word for me."

Tom sucked air through his teeth. "It'll be quite a change."

"I'm ready for it. I've had over three weeks off and can't afford to go through my money too quickly."

Tom winked at his sister. "I can see she's got you well trained already."

Wearing her new going-away outfit, Nell felt as if she was floating as she walked to Windsor Street on Jack's arm. Finally, she was Mrs Jack Riley, and they could spend some time alone together indoors. It would make a change from sheltering at the docks.

"I saw you talking to James earlier. Did he have much to say for himself?"

"Not really. He was asking about the voyage and why we were delayed."

"Why were you? You haven't told me yet."

"No." He paused. "It was just a mix-up in Hong Kong."

"But why did the ship need repairing?"

"It wasn't much, but some heavy winds damaged one of the sails." He smiled at her. "Nothing for you to worry yourself about."

"What did James have to say about it? Did you put him off wanting to go?"

Jack laughed. "No, he seems as keen as ever. Did you know he goes down to the landing stage most days to watch the transatlantic ships?"

Nell's stomach churned. "No, I didn't. Will you have a word with him again? While you were away, he said he was planning to sneak off without telling anyone."

Jack studied her. "Without finishing his apprenticeship?"

Nell nodded. "He doesn't think George will ever agree to him being a steward, and so he won't bother asking for permission. He said he'll just leave one day."

"There's no sense in that." Jack wrapped an arm around Nell's shoulders. "Leave it with me, I'll see what I can do."

Mrs Duffy was waiting for them when they arrived in Windsor Street, and she handed them each a glass of sherry that had been poured and set on the table.

"Congratulations to you both. I made it to the service and very nice it was too."

"I saw you, but I expected you to come back to the house." Jack took a large gulp of his sherry.

"I had things to do, as well you know."

"And we're very grateful. Thank you." Nell smiled, but wasn't sure if a glass of sherry was advisable after all the sloe gin she'd been drinking. After a moment's hesitation, she took a mouthful. *Why not? You only get married once.*

Mrs Duffy sipped her own sherry. "I've sorted the room out for you. I hope you'll be comfortable."

"I'm sure we will." Jack finished his drink. "Now, if you'll excuse us, I think the new Mrs Riley is a little tired."

Nell took another large mouthful of sherry and giggled as Jack escorted her to the bottom of the stairs. "I don't think I should have drunk that so quickly."

"Let me help you, then." He leaned forward and swept her up in his arms. "I need to carry you over the threshold, so I might as well carry you up the stairs, too."

Nell marvelled as he carried her effortlessly up two flights of stairs to their second-floor room.

"Here we are. Home for the time being. I hope you like it."

She nuzzled her face into his neck. "As long as you're with me, I'm sure it will be fine."

Jack pushed the door open with a foot. "My, look at this. I hardly recognise it from the room I left this morning."

Nell got down from Jack's hold and glanced round the room. A large double bed stood against the wall facing them, with a mahogany dressing table and chair in the window. The matching washstand stood neatly in the corner by the wardrobe. It was nice enough.

"Can we use the living room and scullery, too?"

"We can use the front room, but you won't need the kitchen. Mrs D does all the cooking and there's always a pot of tea on the table." Jack ushered her to one side of the bed.

"But what will I do all day?" Nell's brow creased as she

remembered Rebecca's complaints. "It won't take me long to clean in here."

"I'm sure Maria won't mind you giving her a hand. Or you could visit Rebecca."

"I suppose so." She glanced once more around the room. "It's not like having our own house though, is it?"

Jack sat on the bed beside her and planted a kiss on the end of her nose.

"Be patient. Let me settle in at work and then we'll find somewhere of our own. It won't be for long."

A smile brightened Nell's face. "You promise?"

"I promise."

CHAPTER 26

A neat pile of dust sat in the middle of Maria's living room floor as Nell reached over for the dustpan. With a final sweep of the brush, she collected it up and tipped it into the bucket.

"There, that should do it. I'll take this outside and then put the kettle on."

"I'm glad you've been able to come round each day." Maria ran a duster over the fireplace. "It's rather lonely now the two of you have left, not to mention that the house still needs cleaning."

"I don't know how Mrs Duffy manages on her own. She cleans most of the house herself, although I doubt the bedrooms get done as often as we'd like."

"Well, she's no need to do your room, and I bet the other women in the house do their own, too."

"They do, although there aren't many of us. I'm still not used to it."

"You shouldn't be there for much longer."

"I hope not. I'd like my own house, sooner rather than

later. I've been thinking, though. Don't you think it would be nice if we could all live together? For all that they need a place to sleep, the men aren't here very often, between going to work and the alehouse."

Maria stopped and studied her. "What a good idea. It's only you and me who are here all the time. Maybe if we put the money we pay for this place in a pot with the money Jack's paying for your room, we could afford one of those new three-bedroomed houses further down Windsor Street."

"That's what I was thinking. Why don't we get a move on and take a walk down there to see them? I'm sure Jack would be happy."

"George would be too, if we could get a bigger house without it costing him more money." A rare smiled flashed across Maria's lips. "You may have solved all our problems."

Nell's smile faded as she stood by the bedroom window staring out over Windsor Street. She'd been so excited to talk to Jack about the house they'd seen, but he was later than usual and there was still no sign of him. She let out an involuntary sigh. *I hope he's not taken to calling at the alehouse straight from work.* She checked the clock again. Nearly half past six. Mrs Duffy wouldn't be happy; she'd be wanting to get tidied up. Nell turned from the window and made her way to the stairs. She'd have to go down ahead of him.

Mrs Duffy was at the table when she arrived. "No sign of Jack yet?"

"No. I thought I'd better come and apologise for him."

"Oh, don't worry yourself. He told me he'd be late."

"He did?"

Mrs Duffy nodded as Nell took the seat opposite her. "He said he'd forgotten to tell you, so told me instead."

Nell took her seat. "I suppose he left in a hurry this morning…"

"I'm sure he'll be here shortly. I think the last exam was due to end at six o'clock."

"The exam?" Nell stared at the older woman.

"Ah. He didn't tell you that either. I've probably said enough…"

Nell's cheeks coloured. "No, you haven't. I'm grateful that you told me. What exam was it…?"

Mrs Duffy didn't answer as the front door opened and she stood up to walk to the hall.

"Here you are." She ushered Jack into the dining room. "Didn't I tell you he wouldn't be long?"

Jack grinned as he joined them. "Good evening."

"Good evening." Nell raised her head, but immediately returned to studying the tablecloth.

"Why don't you take a seat and I'll bring your tea?" Mrs Duffy held out a chair for him. "I think Mrs Riley wants a word with you."

Jack planted a kiss on Nell's head. "What's the matter?"

"Nothing." Nell kept her head down.

"It doesn't look like nothing."

Nell sat back as Mrs Duffy put two plates of boiled fish and mashed potato onto the table. "Here we are. I'll leave you to have a chat. I'll be in the front room if you need me."

Jack waited for the door to close behind her. "What's going on? She never leaves us on our own."

Nell flaked a piece of fish into her potatoes but couldn't bring herself to speak.

"Nell, please. Tell me what's the matter."

"Your tea will go cold."

He picked up his knife and fork and shovelled a forkful of potato into his mouth. "Have you had a nice day?"

Nell choked and placed her fork on the table. "Why does Mrs Duffy know more about you than I do?"

Jack's brow creased. "What do you mean?"

"She knew you'd be late tonight, while I stood at the window waiting for you."

"Only because I told her to tell you." He cut himself a chunk of fish. "If you remember, I was running late this morning. It was only when I reached the bottom of the stairs, I remembered I hadn't mentioned it."

"Did you want her to tell me about the exam too?"

"Ah."

Nell searched his face, tears threatening to overflow onto her cheeks. "You've taken your first-mate exams, haven't you?"

"It's not what you think." Jack put down his knife and fork and reached for her hand, but she pulled it away.

"You promised you wouldn't go back to sea."

"And I won't, but I did all the work for the exams while we were in Hong Kong, so it seemed silly not to take them. It won't do me any harm."

"But there was no point."

"There *was* a point. It may seem strange, but this will help me in the office too. A first mate's more likely to get a promotion than a second mate."

"In an office?"

185

"Yes, because it shows you're able to learn." He wiped a tear from her cheek. "Why would I want to go away and leave you again?"

"I don't know, but there's more chance you'll be tempted back."

Jack picked up his knife and fork again. "The only thing that would tempt me back is if I became a master mariner and could take you with me."

Nell frowned at him. "But you couldn't do that without going to sea and working as a first mate."

"Exactly. So I won't be doing it."

CHAPTER 27

Nell was at the dressing table, brushing her hair, when the bedroom door opened and Jack burst in.

"My, you're early." She grinned as he kissed the top of her head. "Is this to make up for last night?"

"Not exactly, but I've some news."

"What?" Nell could sense his excitement.

"You're now looking at First Mate Riley. I passed my exams." He thrust a certificate at her. "I'm hoping to get a pay rise out of it, at the very least."

Nell hesitated. "That's good, more money's always welcome. You're sure you don't have to go back to sea to prove yourself?"

Jack put the certificate on the bed and took her in his arms. "How many times do I have to tell you? No! I've seen enough of the world to last a lifetime and I want to be here with you."

Nell's shoulders relaxed. "Will we have enough money to get our own house then, if you get a pay rise?"

Jack smirked at her. "That's the plan. What do you say

about going to see the new houses further down Windsor Street on Saturday afternoon?"

"Oh, yes. They're lovely." Nell's smile returned. "I walked up there with Maria the other day."

"Maria?" His face dropped.

"Well, yes. We were talking about moving and had the idea of moving up there together…"

"Oh, you mean live next door." Jack laughed as he released his hold on her. "I thought for a minute you wanted to share a house with her."

Nell studied the floor. "W-would it be such a bad thing if we did? Live together, that is."

"Why on earth would we do that?" His brow creased. "I thought you wanted us to have our own house?"

"I do … but with you out at work all day, and George and the boys always missing, Maria and I get lonely. We thought we could split the rent between us…"

Jack's smile disappeared. "You've already arranged it?"

"No! I wouldn't do anything without asking you, but we thought we'd be able to afford a three-bedroomed house if we rented it together." Nell glanced up as Jack strode towards the door. "Please don't be angry with me, it was only an idea. We don't have to do that…"

"No, we don't." He pulled open the door. "I'm going to the alehouse for half an hour. I'll see you at tea."

Jack was at the dining table, halfway through a bowl of soup, by the time Nell arrived downstairs.

"Ah, here you are, dear." Mrs Duffy stood up to get Nell

her food. "Jack was telling me about his promotion. You must be so proud of him."

"Yes, I am. Very proud." Nell took her seat and watched Jack dip his bread into the soup.

"Here we are." Mrs Duffy placed a bowl half the size of Jack's in front of her. "I was just saying, if you want to stay here when he goes back to sea, you're more than welcome."

Nell's eyes were wide. "He's ... h-he said that..." Nell struggled to breathe.

"No, I didn't. Mrs D assumed I'd be off again, but I put her right. Didn't I, Mrs D?"

"Maybe you did, but if you change your mind..."

Jack dropped his bread onto the table and sat back in his chair. "What is it with you women that you never believe a word I say?"

"Because you always say things you don't mean." Mrs Duffy gave him a knowing look. "I remember this time last year, you were never going to sea again after you failed your exams."

Bile rose from Nell's stomach. "You'd already failed? Is that why you agreed to give up the sea?"

"No, of course not." Jack glared at his landlady. "Don't you have washing-up to do?"

"There's no need to be like that, I was only being honest." Mrs Duffy snatched his near empty bowl and shuffled out of the room, pulling the door closed behind her.

"So it was nothing to do with me?" Nell fidgeted with her fingers.

"Of course it was." He reached for her hands, but she pulled them away. "Listen, I admit I wasn't proud of myself when I failed last time, that's why I didn't say anything, but

I wasn't serious about giving up the sea until you agreed to walk out with me."

"Then why did you tell Mrs Duffy you were?"

Jack shrugged. "Pride, I suppose. I'd messed up and wanted to pretend it didn't matter."

"But it did." Nell wiped her eyes. "Did you mess up when you promised me you'd stay at home, too? Is that why you slipped off to take your exams without telling me?"

Jack said nothing as Mrs Duffy reappeared and plonked a second bowl in front of him.

"Jam roly-poly."

"Thanks." He sank his spoon into the custard and cut himself a large chunk of sponge as she pulled the door closed.

"I'm sorry, Nell, I just didn't want to upset you."

"Did it ever occur to you that it would have helped if you'd told me about it? The thing that hurts most is that you confided in Mrs Duffy, when you couldn't tell me. I'm not a child, you know."

Jack grinned at her. "I already know that."

"Will you stop treating this as a joke?" Nell stood up and wandered to the fire. "Maria was right, wasn't she? You'll never give up the sea. Not completely. Is that why you married me before you took your exams? To trap me?"

"No." Jack leapt from his chair and took hold of her shoulders. "I married you because I love you. Can't you see that?" Ignoring her protests, he wrapped his arms around her. "I've got myself a job, like you wanted, and hopefully I'll get a pay rise because I passed my exams. You should be happy. I wouldn't have suggested looking for a house if I hadn't planned on staying."

Nell buried her face in his chest. "I'm sorry. I didn't mean to make you angry."

"You didn't make me angry; I was confused why you wanted to live with Maria when we could have a home of our own. You know we don't see eye to eye."

Nell let her tears soak into Jack's shirt. "We don't have to; I don't even know why we thought it was a good idea."

He kissed the top of her head. "Don't cry. When I was in the alehouse, I had a chance to think about what you'd said. I didn't realise you got lonely at home; I thought that was why you have visitors ... or go visiting."

"It is, but, well ... I suppose I'm used to having a big family..."

"All right, let me think about it then." He lifted her chin with a finger and gave her lips a gentle kiss. "I want you to be happy."

Nell wiped her eyes and wrapped her arms around his neck. "I will be if you're with me."

Jack's impish grin returned. "Let's leave this and go upstairs. Mrs D will be itching to come in and tidy up, and I'd rather have you to myself."

Nell lay on the bed and relaxed back into Jack's arms.

"It's so nice to have a room of our own, rather than freezing to death by the docks."

Jack laughed. "It is that, although there were times at sea when I missed the cold English winters."

"Really?"

"When we were in China, it was so hot, your clothes would stick to you from morning to night. The only way to cool down was to jump into the water and hope you didn't take too long to dry out."

Nell smiled as Jack wrapped his arms more tightly around her. "I can't even imagine that."

"I wish I could take you to all these places. You'd love travelling."

"I would." She propped herself up on her elbow. "We still could, though, couldn't we? As passengers."

Jack snorted. "I'd better start saving now, if you want to do that. Have you any idea how much it would cost?"

"No." Nell sank back onto her pillow. "Why does money have to spoil everything?"

"I suppose it needn't." His eyes narrowed as he paused. "Perhaps sharing a house with Maria and the boys wouldn't be such a bad idea if it meant we could save up."

Nell turned back to face him. "Do you mean that?"

"There's no harm giving it a try. I'd love to take you to sea and visit the places I've been to, and if that's the only way we can do it, then why not?"

"Oh, Jack, thank you." Nell's grin was broad. "Can we go to America?"

"If you want to."

She giggled. "Perhaps we could travel on the same ship as James and he can be our steward."

Jack grimaced. "I'm not sure that even living with Maria would be enough for us to go first class."

"Oh." Nell's bottom lip dropped. "So, we'd have to go in steerage?"

"Are you turning me down now?" Jack stroked her cheek.

"Of course not. I'd work on the ship if it meant I could go with you."

Jack smiled. "You know, when I was younger, I used to dream of taking my future wife on voyages with me. Not on the cargo ships, obviously. I imagined that one day I'd make it to master mariner and captain my own passenger ship. I always thought that if I did, I'd take my wife with me."

"Can you do that?"

"Oh, yes. Plenty do." His grin returned. "I used to wonder if they only did it to save renting a house, although I'm sure it's because they liked their wives being with them."

Nell gazed at him. "Maybe it was a bit of both."

"Perhaps." His eyes shifted to the window. "I don't suppose we'll do anything like that now. Even now I'm a first mate, it would take years to become a master mariner."

Nell's eyes narrowed. "Are first mates allowed to take their wives?"

He shrugged. "Possibly. It depends on the ship and the shipping line, and sometimes the captain."

"But there'd be a chance?" Nell stroked his hand. "What do the wives do all day? They can't stay with their husbands."

Jack laughed. "From what I've heard, the captains' wives are usually the most sought-after guests on the ship. Any passenger worth their salt wants to be on good terms with the captain, and what better way for the womenfolk to earn their keep than by befriending the captain's wife."

"And would the wives of a first mate be as popular?"

"I imagine they would be, especially if they spend most

of their time with the captain's wife." Jack raised an eyebrow at her. "What are you thinking?"

Nell cocked her head to one side. "What if I travelled with you as a first-mate's wife?"

"But I won't be working as a first mate, remember. You made me promise."

"Only because I don't want to live without you, but if I could travel with you... That would be different."

Jack sat up straight. "You're serious, aren't you?"

"Why not? I've wanted to go to sea for as long as I can remember."

"But what about Maria and getting a house with her?"

Nell's shoulders sagged before she brightened again. "Maybe we still could. If you earn enough money to pay our share of the rent, we could do that and have somewhere to stay between trips. What do you think?"

"You mean once I've recovered from Maria giving me a bashing for breaking my promise?

"I'd tell her it was my idea, which it is." She stroked a hand down his cheek. "We can't let her stop us if we want to go, and now would be the perfect time, while we've no children." Nell's eyes scanned his. "If I could travel with you now, I'd be happy to wait to be a mam."

"I don't know." He let out a sigh. "You may already be in the family way, and I wouldn't be able to take you with me immediately. I've never worked on a steamship, or a passenger liner ... or as a first mate, so I'd need a few voyages before you could come with me, even assuming the captain would let you. And he might not."

"Oh." Nell pouted as she sank back onto the bed. "Why does something always have to spoil it?"

"I'm sorry." He leaned over and kissed her forehead. "None of these things may happen, I just don't want to raise your hopes."

Nell paused. "How quickly could you move to a passenger ship, do you think?"

Jack shrugged. "I don't know. They're becoming popular, so it may be a while."

"Could you carry on working in Liverpool while you wait? You know, get the house we want and then go to sea when the right offer comes along?"

"I can't make any promises, but if you'd like to come with me, I can make some enquiries. Do you want me to?"

Her smile returned as she held his gaze. "There can't be any harm in asking. Can there?

"It's not the asking that's the problem, it's what it leads to. We need to be sure."

Nell pulled him down on top of her. "The only thing I'm sure of, is that I want to be with you. For the rest of my life."

THE NEXT INSTALLMENT...

The Wife's Dilemma
Liverpool. January 1881

Jack's due back ... and Nell is waiting. She's dreamt of this moment for a long time.

Nine years after their plan was hatched, Master Mariner Jack Riley is ready to take control of his own ship. And Nell is preparing to travel with him.

Counting down the days until he gets home, she longs to see America ... and nobody is going to stop her. Not her two young daughters ... and especially not her sister, Maria.

But when tragedy strikes, her world is thrown into turmoil.

As she comes to terms with her new future, she's given the chance to pursue her dreams.

Should she follow her heart ... or submit to the norms expected of her in Victorian-era, England?

Based on a true story, *The Wife's Dilemma* is Part 2 of *The Windsor Street Family Saga*. A story of love, loss and hope set in Victorian-era Liverpool and beyond.

To get your copy visit
www.valmcbeath.com/windsor-street
or search for VL McBeath at your preferred store.

For details of the rest of the series, including special offers
and new release dates, join my newsletter team at:

https://www.subscribepage.com/fsorganic

If you enjoyed *The Sailor's Promise*, I'd be delighted if you'd
share your thoughts and **leave a review** at your favourite
store.

Finally, for details of other books by VL McBeath, turn to
the next page.

Thank you!

AUTHOR'S NOTE AND ACKNOWLEDGEMENTS

One of the joys of turning my family history research into novels is the way it brings characters and their communities to life.

Back in 2008 when I started my research, I wanted to know more than just the names and important dates related to my ancestors. I was fortunate that the family who became the focus of my initial research led such extraordinary lives. So much so, that many events were covered in the newspapers. Once their story was told (in *The Ambition & Destiny Series*) I was eager to see if there were other ancestors with lives worth writing about.

That was when I stumbled across Nell.

It turned out that her early life was harsh, losing both parents by the time she was six, although given the norms of the time, it probably wasn't particularly unusual. Her sister Maria was thirteen years older, and at the time of their father's death, assuming responsibility for Nell and Rebecca would have been expected. The fact she was already married would have helped financially, too.

As far as Jack was concerned, I was amazed at how much detail was available on genealogy websites. It's true he was a second mate at the start of the book and that he took and passed his first-mate exams within a week of his marriage to Nell. He was also at sea for ten months prior to the marriage.

There was clearly a lot of affection between them given the speed they were married once he came home. But what was life like for Nell while he was away? I imagine that living with her sister and her family would have been quite mundane, but she must have yearned for a family and home of her own.

Did Jack promise to give up his job, though? In truth, I've no idea, but I wondered how keen Nell would be to marry a man who was hardly ever at home. I'm sure I wouldn't like it! That's why, in the absence of any concrete data, I created the story to suggest that she would only walk out with him if he gave up the sea.

So far, so good. A typical girl meets boy type romance, but that's not why I wrote the story.

It was what happened ten years later that intrigued me enough to dig deeper.

Part 2 of the series is *The Wife's Dilemma* and picks up the story nine years later. A year prior to that event.

To order your copy click search for **VL McBeath** at your favourite store.

ALSO BY VL MCBEATH

A Deadly Tonic (A Novella)

Murder in Moreton

Death of an Honourable Gent

Dying for a Garden Party

A Scottish Fling

The Palace Murder

Death by the Sea

A Christmas Murder

To find out more about visit VL McBeath's website at:

https://www.valmcbeath.com/

ABOUT THE AUTHOR

Born and raised in Liverpool (UK), VL McBeath (Val) initially trained as a scientist and worked in the pharmaceutical industry for many years.

It was only more recently she developed a passion for writing.

Her first series, *The Ambition & Destiny Series*, arose out of Val's interest in her family's history. After many years it developed into an epic family saga. Spanning over seventy years, it tells the story of one family's trials, tribulations and triumphs as they seek their fortune in Victorian-era, England.

Once their tale was told, Val was eager to see if there were other ancestors worth writing about. That was when she stumbled across Nell. As a woman living in the late nineteenth century, she was not your typical Victorian housewife, which made her the prefect person to write about. Her story is told in *The Windsor Street Family Saga*.

In addition, to her family sagas, Val also has a series of historical murder mysteries: *Eliza Thomson Investigates*. This is currently a series of seven standalone books set in the early 20th century. Eliza is a fictional amateur sleuth who makes the most of her position being married to the village doctor. Along with her her best friend Connie and occasionally her son, Henry, Eliza likes to help the police with their murder enquiries - whether they want her to or not!

Born and raised in Liverpool (UK), Val now lives in Cheshire with her husband, Stuart. In addition to family history, her interests include rock music, Liverpool Football Club and visiting her two grown-up daughters.

For further information about any of Val's work, visit her website at: **www.vlmcbeath.com**

FOLLOW ME

at:

Website:
https://valmcbeath.com

Facebook:
https://www.facebook.com/VLMcBeath

BookBub:
https://www.bookbub.com/authors/vl-mcbeath

Made in the USA
Middletown, DE
12 April 2024

52952457R00128